Chapter One: You Won't

Dylan looked down into the dark water of the Schuylkill River on the famous Girard Avenue Bridge. This was a bit of a detour from the optimal route back to his home on Parrish street, but Dylan felt he needed to clear his head.

He lost the girl.

He lost *another* good thing.

He **lost**.

It was seemingly the story of young Dylan's tortured— yet exuberant—existence. As he looked down into the murky depths of the polluted water that ran beneath him on that fabled bridge, he could think only one thing. It was actually a voice, seemingly right there upon his shoulder. It was an old, familiar voice. It was shrill, yet unassuming. It was soothing and calming, yet somehow diabolical. It said but one thing.

"Go ahead, man...

... Just do it!"

Dylan was completely alone on the bridge. There were no passers-by for what seemed like miles in every direction. No cars. No people on foot. No stray cats. No rats. Just Dylan and his old friend, or foe. The voice grew louder, almost demanding action from Dylan.

"Go ahead, you piece of shit!

You let her go!

She is too good for you anyway!

You know that, don't you?"

Dylan fought back the best he could. "You don't know **anything**!" he shouted into the darkness. "**Get out of my head!**"

Before he even knew what was happening, Dylan had found his way up onto the ledge that overlooks the Schuylkill.

Now, if you have ever gone swimming in the Schuylkill before, you know a few things about it. One, you know **not to do it**! And if you have, you also likely know what an inner-ear infection feels like. Also, the Schuylkill isn't the Mississippi or anything. That is to say that it is not the most awe-inspiring or majestic river. It is not the widest. Nor is it the deepest. But it certainly is enough to kill someone who never learned to swim.

Dylan never *wanted* to learn how to swim. As he told Jackie that night on Mulholland, he's brilliant. So, he knew **how** to swim. He got the **mechanics** of swimming. He understood the **motions** and the **responsibilities** required to swim. He simply never **wanted** to master it.

"Why would I need to learn to swim? I live on land! I'm not a fucking dolphin! I don't even go to Jersey anymore! So, why bother?"

Also, the fact that he never mastered the art of swimming allowed for the Schuylkill to perhaps be his final resting place.

Yeah. There's that.

As he leaned over the edge, he had one sudden image in his mind. He thought of his mother, Midge, wearing a black skirt that was adorned with lace-flower embellishments and a frilly black shirt with puffed out sleeves. She was also wearing a black veil that hung over her eyes and flowed from a large black formal hat. Her eyes and her face were swollen and drenched in tears. She leaned over an open casket. She kissed the young man in the casket and broke down again.

"You know I will follow you, Dylan!" she screamed as she sobbed violently over her youngest's lifeless body. "I'll see you soon!"

At this thought, Dylan stepped down from the ledge. Though she would never know it, Midge saved Dylan yet again that night. Yes, not as obviously or heroically as she had done when he was seven and fell into the 12-foot-deep end of the in-ground pool at Uncle Gordon's chateau, the site of a family function.

On **that** day, she sprang into action. She dove head-first into the pool and swam quickly and gracefully to salvage and rescue Dylan. She was like **David**

Hasselhoff that day. Okay, maybe she was like a **dolphin**, not **the Hoff**. Or maybe some hybrid of the sort? Like a David Hassel-**dolph**? On that day, she showed Dylan exactly what it means to love someone.

See, Midge had a chronic inner ear infection, so she had to avoid swimming at all costs. On the rare occasion that she went into the water when the Stewart boys were younger, Midge would suffer through the coming night, occasionally for days on end that followed, as she struggled to ease the immense, almost insufferable discomfort that is caused by inner-ear infections and water-logged ears. Can you guess how a young Midge obtained her chronic inner-ear infection? Yes, you guessed it. Her and her siblings would swim in the Schuylkill on hotter days. It was a giant pool for poor kids.

Dylan loved his mother. He could never take his own life. He couldn't fathom doing that to her. At that moment, he thought, again, of the night with Jackie at the Hollywood sign.

"You gotta live for **you**, Dylan! That is the only way out of this mess you're in! You gotta **own your life**, man!"

It was that advisement from Jackie that made Dylan roll-up his sleeves upon his return to Philly and do what he needed to do. In that way, and in so many ways she now may never know, Jackie *saved* Dylan from himself. From his own bullshit. What could he do without her, though?

Dylan returned home to find Midge wide awake in the living room. She was watching Married With Children. It was the Supermarket Sweep episode, where Al and Peggy are playing a game of "Supermarket Sweep" against Marcy and Jefferson Darcy. Dylan loved this episode. He remembered watching it with Midge when it aired in 1991. He had not yet turned 8 years old. Dylan went over to Midge and stood in front of her. In doing so, he blocked the television. She seemed to be bothered by this and craned her neck to see around and past him. She stopped doing that when she saw that Dylan looked forlorn. She then turned off the TV and spoke up. "What's wrong, Dylan?"

"Nothing," he said, and then corrected himself. "Well, everything, mom."

"It's that Jackie, right?"

"Yeah, I mean…" He was confused. "How did you know?"

"I know everything, Dylan!" She locked eyes with him and continued. "Remember when I hid in the dumpster behind Masterman when you were twelve? I heard you swearing and breaking shit?"

"Yeah, you're a looney toon," Dylan said while laughing. He then got very serious with his mother.

"I want you to know how much I appreciate you, mom! I know I'm a *bit* of a prick sometimes!"

"**All** the time, Dylan! **All the time!**"

"I wouldn't say *all* the time, but I get *prick-ish* sometimes..."

He then pivoted the conversation back to a more serious place. "She went back to LA today and I tried to catch her, but I missed her train. I don't know what to do. She won't even pick up the phone."

"Dylan, she made up her mind. I'm sorry, kid. There isn't anything left to do."

"I know, mom, I know. I just..." Dylan realized then that he was in this alone, and he didn't like that feeling.

"I'll be fine. Thanks mom."

As Dylan walked away from the couch and climbed the stairs, Midge called to him again. "I love you, Dylan. Just focus on school."

"I know. I love you too, mom!"

I don't want to focus on school! I hate school! I hate every choice I ever made! **Fuck***!*

As Dylan lay in bed, he looked at his phone again, and it filled him with even more crippling dread. He was certain he would never see Jackie again. And it **killed** him inside. Just then, he heard a familiar voice coming from next to him.

"You shoulda just jumped in!...

...What are you *doing*?

...You **think** you'll be ok?

...**You** won't."

Chapter Two: Sangry (The Children of Cyber Frank Wychek)

"You gotta cut your shit, dude!" Kay said.

He was in rare form today. He continued to his younger brother. "She went back because you told her a girl blew you. Correct me if I'm wrong, but a **good** friend encourages— nay, **celebrates** that. She seems like a dick friend to me, dude!"

"I broke her heart, man. I had no idea she—"

"Liked you?! Well, she came 3,000 miles just to see you, so that seems like a pretty good confession to me," Kay said, before noticing that he had affected Dylan with that evaluation, which he then quickly attempted to walk back. "But, hey, she's a grown up. She can use her words. She should have said something sooner! That isn't on you, brother."

"I know, man, I know. I just wish I would've known sooner!"

"I know, dudenstein, but you didn't. What are ya gonna do? Just move forward, Dylan. She's gone."

Dylan received that grim realization from his brother and quickly changed the topic of the conversation.

"So, you almost done?"

Kay looked back over his shoulder to see if his manager was paying close attention, which he wasn't. He leaned in closer to Dylan over the counter at Sears, and spoke in a low, muddled tone, saying, "I'm gonna tell Skeet there's a family medical thing. It should be fine. Just do me a favor?"

"Yeah, shoot."

"Act like you're worried about something. Bust out your acting chops, but **don't oversell the part**. Just a

13

believable, **slight** panic?" he said, with a real sway in his voice. "Can you do that for me?"

Dylan enjoyed acting. It was the real reason he was so serious about backyard wrestling. It gave him the stage on which to act out fantasies. Really, just to **be** someone else, even for just a few hours at a time. He obviously relented to Kay's request. Dylan then put a slight grimace on his face. Nothing too over-the-top, as Kay had requested. Dylan posed to himself the age-old question of an actor preparing for a role—

What's my motivation?

For this part, Dylan projected himself to be a young man who needed his brother to accompany him to their home to help to feed their invalid mother. This fictional parent suffered through a metastasized cancer in her bowels. The progress of her recovery had stalled quite a bit in the winter months, and both brothers were worried that she might not make it to Groundhog Day. Her limbs had become almost useless in her state, and her appetite was understandably not what her doctors had hoped that it would be. Their fictional father was a police officer who died in the line of duty in 1995. Since his death, she had become ultra-dependent upon her boys for support. And since her cancer diagnosis in '97, the brothers were almost breaking under the immense weight of supporting the once strong-willed woman who gave them both life on earth.

As Dylan thought of his "motivation," a single tear slid down his cheek. He looked to the window near the front of the store and his eyes found the distance. He shook his head slightly as he got lost in the scene, as though he was thinking about what life was going be like without his fictional invalid mother. He then felt a hand on his shoulder. It was Kay, getting his attention.

"Alright, come on, man."

I'd like to thank the academy...

Dylan turned to face his brother, and as he did, he noticed the manager looking at Dylan and Kay.

The show must go on.

Dylan then quickly got back into character. He turned toward the exit of the store and began talking in a hurried tone, "Okay, we gotta hurry. I'm sorry to spring this on you like this!"

As they reached the exit to the store, Dylan noticed that the manager was no longer watching them, and Kay was laughing quietly. Dylan smacked his brother's shoulder playfully. "Ya fuckin' dick!"

Kay then raced the conversation to a discussion of a plan.

"So, what do you wanna do now that I'm out?" he asked, before adding a classic Kay clarification of their pending itinerary. "No **gay** shit!"

Rare form.

"I dunno, man. I think I'm gonna go back to Hollywood soon."

Kay looked like he had just witnessed a grown man kick a puppy. That is to say he appeared to be both angry as well as sad. Sangry, if you will.

"How the **fuck** are you gonna do that, dude? Let's see the checklist... A. Temple, which is finally going your way. And you're almost a sophomore now! B. Money, of which you have none, with no prospect for future monies. Oh and C. Mom, who will fucking destroy you if you *even* consider this."

Good points. All of them.

Kay then continued ."And D. Your brother Kay. What the **fuck** am I gonna do, dude?"

"I dunno. I just can't keep feeling like this. I know that people say all the time that bad stuff gets better. And shit gets easier. But I don't want to just move on from this one, Kay." Dylan said with sadness brimming to the surface, "I **can't** let her go."

When the Stewart boys entered their house, they found Midge sitting on the couch. She appeared to be eating a Hot Pocket while watching a rerun of Frasier. It was the one where Roz tells Martin to move in with Niles, because Frasier and Martin bicker incessantly and need a break from each other. Niles agrees to the arrangement, because Daphne will also be moving in to Niles' place. When she later decides that she is no longer needed there, because Martin seems to be doing just fine there on his own, Niles kicks out his cane, making him fall. This leads to Daphne remaining, and Frasier spills the hunch that Niles did it in purpose, albeit subconsciously. This leads to immense panic and paranoia between Martin and Niles. Though it was one of Dylan's favorite episodes, he was not in the laugh-out-loud sort of mood, so he and Kay retired to the upstairs.

Dylan and Kay played Madden '02 on PlayStation 2. They had started a franchise together earlier that month. Though they rarely actually played the games, they mutually shared an intense love for the franchise they started. They both did their best to be the magnificent general managers that they had always dreamed they could one day be. If ever given the opportunity, that is.

"You can't go to LA, dude," Kay started in as he shifted the controller from one hand to the other, "**The Titans need you!**"

I can't stay here because of a fucking video game!

Kay continued. "**Frank Mother-fucking Wychek**, dude! Think about **that!**"

He has you there, man! What about the little Wycheks that Frank has at home?

Dylan reached a decision that night. It had nothing to do with Kay. Not even Cyber Frank Wychek or his imaginary cyber children.

"I'm going back. Keep this between us, man."

Stunned silence. Then, Kay spoke up. "**How**?"

"I'll hitchhike if I gotta," Dylan admitted, followed by a long, uneasy pause. "I'd even Forrest Gump it there, I just *gotta* see her."

"Yea, alright, dude," Kay said dismissively as he hoisted the controller back up to search for a free agent tight end for his 49ers franchise, then continued. "It'll be our secret."

"I'm serious, bro," Dylan said with confidence. "I'll check back in when I get there."

Chapter Three: Fucking Skitch! (Journey Out West)

As Dylan walked along the side of an unfamiliar road, he felt a cold, wet drip on his exposed nose. It was very cold outside, which made sense considering that he had now found his way to...

...well, to be totally honest, he had no idea where he was right now. He had been trekking by foot for about 8 or 9 sun-ups now, as he was expecting to see another cloud-covered daytime sky soon. He knew that his family was likely freaking out back on Parrish Street, except he was confident that Kay had likely spilled the beans by now.

Dylan packed light for the trip; just his satchel containing two outfits, his discman, a smaller book of mixed CDs that he had specifically made for this journey the night of his escape from Philadelphia. And obviously his discman. Oh. And AA batteries. **Lots and lots** of AA batteries. He had stopped listening to music earlier in the night, as he wanted to pay closer attention to his surroundings. This happened as he walked through a seemingly crime-dampened borough near what appeared to be Springfield, Ohio. He thought he had seen Nelson Muntz while there, but he was probably mistaken.

No matter. It had been what seemed like 2 or 3 days since he crossed the Ohio/Indiana border. Wayne County seemed nice enough, though he was bitter about how far he was from the Golden Goose.

That's the plan. Get to the Golden Goose. Get a beer from Jackie. Listen to some tunes. Make everything right. Go back home.

He seemed to have it all figured out. By now, the sky had opened up, at least a little bit. It wasn't rain. It was too cold for rain. But it wasn't snow either. It was the wintry mix bullshit that **John Bolaris** always hated so much, before his misfire on the "storm of the century" in February, of course. Dylan was having a hard time seeing the dark road ahead of him, but was assisted by the lights of trucks that were still zooming past him on Interstate 70.

As he walked, the idea to ask for help struck him. He walked slower and drifted toward the pull off lane, and raised his thumb out to his side. As he did this, he brought his walking to a stop.

Maybe someone will take mercy on me 'cause of the conditions.

Yeah. That was the hope.

After probably ten or twelve minutes standing with his hitchhiker thumb out in the cold air, an 18-wheeler approached slowly, with hazard lights blinking, and reflecting off of and through the precipitation.

Please don't be a murderer.

The middle-aged curmudgeon who was occupying the large cabin of the tractor leaned over across the passenger's side and called out of the opened window. "Need a ride?"

No. I just thought it might be cool to let my thumb feel the breeze of the traffic tonight.

"Oh, yeah, man! Thank you!"

"Where are you headed?" the trucker asked.

"I'm actually going to Hollywood."

"Oh, LA. That's home away from home for me. I'm not going all that way, but I can get you much closer."

"Oh, that's great, man! Where are you cutting your commute?"

"I'm taking her to Albuquerque. You'll be way closer there." He then changed his angle. "So, why you going to Hollywood? Nothing is real there, man!"

Wow. Deep advice, pal.

"Yeah, I know, I know. I'm going for a girl."

Vin Diesel laughed heartily. "You know they got girls in Indiana. Yeah, they're not Hollywood elites, or pin-ups or anything, but they got a good stock of 'em here!"

The fuck?

"No, I know, man. I'm going to chase after a girl that left me in Philly. I gotta find her!"

"Wow, that's some crazy shit, dude! She must be pretty special! So, you walked all the way here from there?"

Dylan realized how crazy he must have sounded to this friendly loner.

"Yeah, man. I just had no other choice. She could be the girl of my dreams, sir! What do you call this?"

Vin spoke up with what seemed like admiration. As he smiled and shook his head lightly, he said, "I think that's love, buddy."

Yeah.

Love.

Maybe I can finally have what dad has in mom.

"So, you've been walking for what, 10 days?"

"Yeah, I guess...give or take."

Brother-trucking Love was amazed at this dedication as he inquired further, "When was the last time you slept, man?"

Wow. sleep. Let's see...

"I slept a few hours on a bus stop bench outside of West Mifflin, PA. Then again in a truck stop near Zanesville, Ohio," Dylan said, then chuckled and nodded. "I'm getting by, man!"

"Wow, you must be wrecked! There's a latch on the bottom side there on your right if you wanna kick it back and take a few."

Dylan hesitated slightly at the thought of being asleep in a strange person's big rig in the middle of nowhere. But as he thought of this fear, his eyes grew so heavy that he gave in.

"Don't worry man. I'll let you sleep. I'm not trying to steal anyone's shit or anything. Go ahead man! You're good."

"Thanks buddy. What's your name? I'm Dylan," he said as he reached out his hand for a shake.

"Oh," the trucker reciprocated the handshake gesture, extending his big bear-paw that was cloaked in a black and grey driving glove, "I'm Vince."

Get the fuck...

...Vince?!

...As in "my friend, Michelle Rodriguez calls me Vin?!"

Dylan gripped the hand and shook it. "Nice to meet you, Vince. Thanks, pal. I'm gonna doze off for a bit."

"'K, I'll wake you when we get close to a rest stop. We'll stop in Tulsa, I gotta fuel up and probably take a shit."

"K, man. I'll get grub for us there. Night, dude!"

At this Dylan reclined his seat. He fell harder than he had ever fallen into the unknown abyss of slumber right then and there. He almost immediately was walking out of the record store in Hollywood. He saw the bright lights of Jackie's blue Camaro. He got in and they were off. The car didn't take the usual route that it had when she took him back to his hotel. Instead, she had driven him to a beach. The two then walked on the beach and stared out at the sea for what seemed to be an eternity. The sky then grew darker, and Dylan saw his father on a boat out in the harbor. Dylan called and called and called, but his father's boat just continued to drift out to sea. Dylan then felt a hand nudging his leg. He looked over at Jackie. Her hands were accounted for. It was not her. This scared Dylan, at least for a moment. He then rushed out of this world, and he was suddenly laying in the cabin of the big rig. The hand was Vincent Diesel waking him to tell him they had arrived in Tulsa.

"Wake up, sleepy head," Vincent said. He then laughed as he continued. "You were on that **deep** nocturnal shit!"

K, don't be weird, dude!

"You were having some dream, man. For a long time, you were calling out. Who is Lara?"

Lara?? No, Jackie!

The truck star continued. "Is Lara the Hollywood gal?"

"No, she's Jackie. The girl I'm going to see....is Jackie!"

"Well, then, who is Lara?? Cause you sounded like you were crying or something when you were calling for her. I was gonna wake you up, but I didn't want you to murder me or anything. So I let you work it out, whatever it was."

"Don't worry about it, man. I'm fine. I'll be right back. I'll get us some hot dogs and sodas. Cool?"

"Yeah, that's great, man. Thanks. Ketchup on one, mustard on the other, relish on both. K?"

"Totally, man. Go take a dump and come back, I'll get the grub and wait for you out front of the truck."

Dylan then got the hot dogs, and two large Coca-Colas. As he filled the second 44-ounce cup, he thought of his father's words of warning.

"You can't keep eating and drinking like you do, man! You're gonna die of a heart attack. It's what we Stewart men do! Except Johnny Dark! That fucker eats lean and is gonna live til' he's 200!"

Dylan then put the cap on the soda, collected his goods and went to pay. He saw that Vince Diesel had finished in the bathroom and was waiting at the door of the A&P for Dylan.

Such a nice guy! Toretto...

After they returned to the truck, the two devoured their meals and made small talk about their lives. Dom Toretto lived with his wife just outside of Los Angeles County. He got into trucking because his wife and he started planning for children when they first wed in the summer of '79. Turned out that Vince had been shooting blanks after working at a radiation plant in his twenties. Because of this, they couldn't have children of their own. That didn't stop sir Vinny Diesel-truck though. They adopted a small boy from the impoverished area of southeastern Inglewood, California. That was 1984. The small boy was now running for mayor of a city in Southern California, and he gave all of the credit for how he turned his life around to his father and mother.

This guy is incredible.

This guy reminds me so much of daddy.

Before long, they pulled into a rest stop near Albuquerque, New Mexico.

"Alright, man. We're here. Now, just keep on til' you get to Jackie. Don't you ever give up on her. Ever. It's what your *dad* would do, man!"

"Thanks Vince! You saved my life, dude!"

"Oh, stop it dude. It's been fun!"

Vince had told Dylan that Albuquerque was about 800 miles from LA, give or take. It would still be a bitch to walk, especially through Arizona, where there are coyotes and shit. It was Vince's advice for Dylan to hitch another ride with someone. He suggested asking around at the rest stop where they parted ways, because there were a ton of truckers heading to Los Angeles with their freight.

That is just what Dylan did, and after three or four failed attempts on his part, he found a ride straight to the port of Los Angeles. Then he could get a taxi to the Golden Goose from there. The driver that Dylan found was actually a rather scary dude. Dylan felt fortunate that Vince was basically the polar opposite of this gentleman. His name was Skitch. When Dylan made the obnoxious joke about his name, and if it was on his birth certificate, it was not received well.

"No, it's not. I ain't got no birth certificate, boy."

No birth certificate. Wow.
Charming.

"Look, I know you don't know me from a yam in a casserole, but I'm gonna be with you the next twelve hours or so, and I really do wanna hear about you, Skitch."

It seemed to Dylan that no one had ever wanted to hear Skitch's side of things before, 'cause he just **opened up**. The next several hours were as uncomfortable as they were long.

Turns out, Skitch was delivered in a trailer home and was left in a shoe box on the side of a dirt road in rural Wyoming. His mother was a sex worker at rest stops in the area, and he was the product of her being raped. Skitch was expelled from school at the age of 8 for stabbing another student with a sharpened ruler. Yes.

A shiv.

Fashioned by a second grader.

Rural America.

'**Murica**, if you will.

Skitch did time in juvenile hall until he was released at 17. He then fell in love with a tattoo artist outside of Sedona, Arizona. She cheated on him with a drug dealer there, and he stabbed the dealer in the face with a butter knife, covered in butter from Skitch's cornbread for breakfast. Skitch was then in county lock-up for 2 years, until the charges against him were mysteriously dropped, and he was free to go. Skitch then did the only thing he could, with no education and no prospects. He started driving large trailers for cartels on the Mexican/Arizonian border. Eventually, Skitch met a born-again Christian who took him under his wing. He showed him the many positive things that he could do with his strong will to survive.

    Skitch turned over a new leaf. He started driving trucks for long-haul companies in the western US. He now owned a house outside of Reno, Nevada , which he shared with his wife of six years. Her name was Chandra. They had a one-year old baby girl.

    Skitch slowed down the tractor on the Mojave Expressway near Barstow, California, and pulled out his brown leather wallet. He flipped it open to expose a picture of a beautiful baby girl, crawling on what appeared to be Skitch's chest and belly. The picture was taken from above him, as he lay on the floor and allowed his daughter to investigate the terrain.

"There's my **whole** world, pal!"

"Oh, shit! She's beautiful!" Dylan chose these words, not because he thought she was beautiful. Heavens no, Dylan thinks that all babies are inherently gross. Their heads and faces are still forming, so they are all gross and misshapen. I mean, he loved the **idea** of a baby being cute! It is cute to **consider** babies **being** babies. Babies **existing**. **That is cute**. The idea that this grizzled roughneck who refused to give his actual name is actually a caring, attentive father? **That** is **CUTE!**

Not babies.

Babies are gross.

Also, Dylan didn't want to be stabbed today, so he played nice.

Before long, Dylan was excited to see a sign that read "Port of Los Angeles: ahead, next right."

I made it!

Praise be!

Praise be?

Fucking Skitch!

"Alright, my man! It's been real. Remember. If Jesus wants you to be with Jackie, it will be so! Trust it to be so. Trust in Him! Be good, my man!"

Be well! *Unless you are **demanding** that I be **well behaved**! That would be '**be good**'. If you are wishing me good tidings on my journey, that is "**Be well!**"*

Fucking Skitch!

Chapter Four: Dozer and The Goose (A Much Blacker Hogan Than Hogan)

"I'm telling you, man, I don't know what I'm even doing here, but I gotta do what I gotta do," Dylan said to the driver as they approached Hollywood Boulevard.

"Well, your story sounds like a Hollywood romance to me, buddy! Don't worry. If she doesn't love you yet, she *will* when she sees you and hears what you went through to get to her," Tony Atlas-Cab said in a reassuring tone. "Trust me. Hollywood girls **eat** that kinda shit for a **fourth meal!**"

The taxi slowed down at the corner across from the Golden Goose. Dylan paid the 102-dollar cab fare—evidence to him that a better life must cost more money—and got out. As he did, Tony called out to him in a friendly, exuberant voice, "Good luck brother man! **You'll get her!**"

"Thanks, Tony!"

Dylan crossed a crowded Hollywood Boulevard 'til he found his way through the crowd of customers standing in front of and around the door. It was a Thursday night. Dylan remembered hearing Jackie say that she always worked on Thursdays because Thursdays were a very busy, "college" night there. He maneuvered his way through the crowd and entered the busy bar. He looked around the bar for women wearing tight red tops and short black miniskirts, as that was the waitstaff attire for female employees of the Golden Goose.

Upon scouring the front room, he saw no sign of Jackie, but he knew that he didn't bump into her in the outer room. She had been working in the area of the main bar that night. He started his trek there. There were so many young people in attendance that night. He wondered if there was a band appearing there that evening, or if this was the usual turnout for a Thursday that Jackie spoke of so bitterly when they first met in October.

Dylan made his way to the entrance of the main room of the Golden Goose, playfully referred to as "The Nest."

Fucking Hollywood!

Upon entry, Dylan was greeted by a cheerfully pleasant hostess who stood behind an oak podium.

"Hello! Welcome to the Goose's Nest! Are you here to see the Come-Up-Ins?!"

"No. I don't know them. Are they any good?"

"Yeah! They're a super fun band. They aren't really the most gifted musicians or anything, but they are so full of charm, it's scary! You'll love 'em!" Clarissa said, as she sure did **explain it all** to Dylan. "They go on at 8:30."

"Yeah, maybe I'll check em out," he said as he quickly got to the purpose of his appearance there that evening. "Is **Jackie** working tonight?"

Clarissa looked very perplexed at his inquiry, and shot back, "Who is Jackie?"

"**Jackie**....she's *yea*-big" (he gestured with his hand to the height he remembered Jackie to be) "...she has big sparkling blue eyes, rosy cheeks, the whole nine yards. She normally works on Thursdays, that's why I'm here."

Clarissa responded with what sounded like sincere concern for his well-being, as she started. "I'm sorry, babe. We don't got no Jackies here."

In that moment, Dylan thought back to the night he met Jackie. It was seemingly a lifetime ago now. When they met back in October, he **adored** how she made certain to speak in as close to the Queen's English as she could, at least while still being taken seriously in social terms. Dylan thought then that it was an LA thing versus a Philly thing. That is until Clarissa—if that **is her real name**—just chewed up that response and regurgitated it onto the floor by Dylan's feet. He actually missed his father in that moment, but that thought was short-lived, as Dylan searched his brain for conversations he had with Jackie on his second night in LA, when she was venting about hating her job.

*"When I started there, I didn't even give them my **real** name. I didn't want **anyone** to know me there, and their hiring policies were so lax that we didn't need proof of identity or anything. I know it seems odd, but it's a Hollywood thing."*

That **has** to be it. Now, what is her **fake** name?? What else did she tell you?

"I always loved Christine Lakin. She was 'Al' from *Step By Step,* remember that show? Yeah, she was always an idol of mine. But idols are a dime-a-dozen when you grow up in the LA area. It probably isn't anything like growing up in a big city on the east coast, that's for sure."

Maybe that's it.

"Do you have a Christine here?" Dylan asked with hope in his voice.

"We actually have two," Clarissa said, before reaching for the phone next to her and pivoting. "What did you say your name was?"

"Oh, sorry. I-I-I'm Dylan," he said, while extending a handshake her way. "Dylan Stewart from Philadelphia."

"Philly, eh?" Clarissa asked, with judgment brimming from her lips. "What do you have to do with Christine? And which Christine?"

"I **described** her already."

"Yeah, you described just about every young girl in this town. Or at least you described what I'm sure Philadelphians think they all look like here. Let me guess? Giant tits? No waist?"

"No, no, well... they're **big**, but I wouldn't characterize them as **giant**," Dylan said, as the wheels were seemingly running off of this conversation. "They're supple."

Smooth, Dylan. Smooooooth!

"Sir, I'm gonna have to ask you to leave," Clarissa said while stepping back, with the phone pressed to her ear. She continued on. "If you're not here for the Come-Up-Ins performance, you can't be here."

"Okay... Clarissa?" said Dylan, as he leaned in to feign an effort to read her name tag. "I don't mean any harm at all. I hitchhiked here, which took almost two weeks to do, but I am here. I just want to find Jackie, or Christine, or whatever name she goes by."

"OK, pal," a deep voice behind Dylan's right shoulder bellowed in his direction. It was a large gentleman with arms the size of Hogan's. "It's time to step out. C'mon now."

His name was Charles. He actually once lived in Delaware County, which is just to the south and west of Philadelphia. Charles was a long-time professional wrestler in Delco. He actually had gotten his start in the independent wrestling circuit in the state of Delaware, but had relocated to the Drexel Hill area where he started wrestling for a local fed there. He became a well-respected backstage presence in an industry where that kind of gentleman's position was *so* important. "Dozer" (like **BULL-**) was his *heel persona*, and he would often be the guy who reigned furious blows down upon the helpless fan-favorite referee, only to be thwarted by up-and-coming "baby face" personas. Dozer was so well respected in the local circuit, that he handled the "booking" for almost every federation he was in. As the "booker," he was responsible for scripting the story lines. To his credit, he never booked himself as the top draw. "Always the bad-ass, never the champ," as the saying goes.

Dozer moved out to the Los Angeles area to become an in-demand bouncer at many Hollywood nightlife hotspots. He still wrestled independently, on the side, and used the contacts he made during his night gig to advance his in-ring professional career. On this night, he received the page from sweet Clarissa, with her made-for-TV looks and sweet Georgia accent, for assistance with a troublemaker from Philadelphia.

*What in the **aerial fuck**!*

"I'm not doing anything, sir. I'm just looking for a friend who works here."

"What's her name?" Dozer 'James Earl Jones'-ed at Dylan.

"Jackie. Well, well, not Ja... she told me Ja... but..." As Dylan spewed whatever was racing into his head out at Dozer, it dawned on him that he was blowing whatever chance he had at explaining this obvious clear misunderstanding, and he noticed that the dimly lit room was beginning to close in on him. He was almost cheek to cheek with Clarissa now, it seemed, anyway, as he then, in frustration with the situation, raised his voice at Dozer, which is an obvious mistake.

"Her name is **Jackie! She told me Jackie!** But now, it might be Christine. Yeah, **try Christine... Christine Lakin!**"

"Alright, let's go, man," Dozer said as he grabbed Dylan by the collar and wrestled him into the outer room. Dylan had never been forcibly removed from anywhere before.

It wasn't his favorite pastime.

As they struggled their way to the door, Dylan was pleading his case, as on-lookers snickered and sneered at Dylan like he was worthy of their disdain.

Fucking Hollywood!

"I'm not trouble, man! I came all the way from Philly and it's a Thursday and she said she always works Thursdays," he continued in futility. "**Come on man! Please**? I'm in **love with her** and I **fucked it all up!**"

At this, they had reached the open front door of the Golden Goose, and Dozer picked Dylan up over his head. "Have a good night, sir! Come back soon!" he said as he threw Dylan **literally** out into the street. Now, that had to be a solid 8 or 10 feet from the mat at the door of the Goose. This guy **was** Hogan!

...Well, a much **blacker** Hogan than Hogan, that's for sure.

Chapter Five: What's the Worst That Can Happen??

"Hey, boy! Wake up! You in my spot!" a grizzled war veteran shouted as he nudged Dylan's backside with his worn-down, white and teal Asics.

Just then, Lara stood up from her stool and walked over to answer the door to room 204. A grim specter like something out of Dylan's darkest excursions into horror entered the room. He carried with him an old, battered hatchet. As he entered the classroom, he grabbed the handle with both hands, and began to raise it.

Before anything of consequence played out, Dylan rather abruptly awoke to the sound of **Gus** giving him shit for stealing his prized sleeping spot under an overpass of the 101. Dylan stood up quickly, collected his things, and turned away. Before he did, he addressed this **Jeff Garcia** imposter who was footing his ass cheeks.

"I'm sorry, man. I didn't see a **name** on it or anything. My bad."

Gus laughed heartily, then answered back. "If **you** gonna make it out here, you need to learn a few things. First thing first, learn respect." He continued, "Cause quick-lip gon' get you stabbed, son!"

Dylan changed the pace and mood of this discussion as he responded to the wise musings of G.I. Gus. "Look, man. I'm sorry. I'm not even **from** here. I came from Philly for a girl and got thrown out of a bar tonight. I'm here with no money, no food, no prospects, **nothing**. Well, I have two outfits, and my music."

"That's way more'n I had for 8 years, bcy!" Gus said with forlorn angst. "I got a TBI in Kuwait in '91. I los' my house, ma' car, ma' family."

Dylan immediately thought of the hair band Poison. He felt bad that as Gus continued his discussion of his real-life hardships, Dylan kept hearing Bret Michaels' agonizing lyrics about a "suicidal Vietnam vet." He did his best to shake the image of the classic "Something To Believe In" video on MTV and began listening again, at least to what he still caught of the tale.

"... memory, and bad fucking headaches. I can't stay straight long 'nuff to work a job. So, I'm out here."

"Holy God, I'm sorry, man!"

"God? **HA!**" Gus shouted with clear contempt for the thought. "Der' ain't no damn God, boy! You won't know until you know. I hope you don' ever fin' out."

"You can't say that, man!" Dylan said, with sincere hope in his voice. "I met a man on my way here who was on a fast track to horror, and he told me he was taken in by a born-again, and it totally changed his

whole life. He has a **wife** and **child** and **everything.** All I'm saying is, you never know."

"Well, that is good for him, but it ain't worth a hill of beans for me! There ain't no one watching out for me from up-on-high, buddy! We are **all** in this alone." Gus spat his disdain for the almighty back at Dylan. "And, look, if you gonna survive out here, you need to understand that there ain't nobody in this but you, for you. It's you. Only you."

What kinda Peter Klett shit is this?!

Dylan loved Candlebox and all, but he quickly changed the topic. "I appreciate the thoughts, man. Can you suggest a sleeping spot for me for the first night out here?"

"Well, yea, not here!" Gus laughed back at him.

Fucking Gus Ferotte!

Gus continued. "Yeah, you can try... uh... yeah, 'ere's a park right up by Lexington n' Wilton that got good cover. You can try 'ere..."

"Oh, thanks man! I'll be around, if you need to chat or whatever, I gotchu Gus! Stay warm tonight!"

"Alright, man. You too. Solid."

Solid? Vagrancy lingo is tricky.

Dylan then made his way back to street-level, so he could began his brisk evening trek to the park on Lexington. He found his way, and it occurred to Dylan that Gus really knew his stuff. This park was practically the homeless Four Seasons! I mean, there likely wasn't a turn-down service, or continental breakfast, or a cocktail cabinet fridge, but, **when in Rome...**

Dylan laid his satchel full of clothes on a park bench to be utilized as a pillow for the night. He never expected to be sleeping outside before two weeks ago, but now it seemed that he was becoming a seasoned vagrant. It filled him with a sense of misguided pride.

Or something.

He suddenly felt the tug of panic within him. He knew that he must reach home to tell his mother where he was and when he will be home. However, he struggled with that a bit. See, Dylan had no intention of leaving LA this time. Well, not until he saw Jackie again and made things right with her. If only he could explain that to his mother. She would **have** to understand. She basically **wrote the book** on stupid, "old-timey" love. She would be so *proud* of him for not letting **anything** stand in the way of connecting with his one true love.

Fuck!

*It sounds **so** damned good!*

He then took out his phone. He dialed Jackie. After three and a half rings, Jackie sang "I Almost Forgot," said her peace, and then the beep. Dylan spoke up, his growing lack of confidence showing in the quivering of his voice as he spoke.

"Jackie. I'm sleeping at the park on Lexington and Wilton tonight. I hitchhiked to visit you, but you weren't in tonight, and Charles, the bouncer, threw me onto my asshole onto the street. Ah..." he sighed, "Uh, I- I... I don't care, I'm gonna try again tomorrow."

Dylan then said, with a feeling of fear-of-consequence gripping his innards, "Maybe he'll go easier on me next time?"

Dylan's voice began to crack, as he felt a deep stinging pain.

...In his soul.

He then kept on. "I love you, Jackie! I know it! Please talk to me? **Please**?!"

Dylan paused for effect, then delivered, with reverence and pain-staking regret: "I'm so sorry, kiddo!"

He hung up the phone. He looked at it again. He considered calling home to Midge and Sam and his brothers.

What will I say?

He put the phone back in his pocket and closed his eyes. As he lay there, he thought to himself.

What's the worst that can happen?

Chapter Six: Where'd you go?

Dylan was in a panic, searching as he approached the entrance to the Golden Goose. For the first time he could remember, the blackest Hogan was not guarding the door and performing his cursory identification checks there. Dylan entered hastily and made his way inside. Now, he knew he would need to do his own reconnaissance mission to uncover Jackie's known whereabouts. In that moment, he thought of his old pal Skitch's journey to religious enlightenment.

*If ever I need **God's** help, it is now. Please, **oh please** show me Jackie? I'm **begging** you, Lord above.*

Dylan knew he had to avoid Clarissa at all costs, as she was the stuck-up whistleblower who dropped the dime on his previous attempt at the Goose.

How can I find her without involving staff?

He thought about things that Jackie had told him about her employment. Tricks of the trade that she uncovered during her bitter time there.

*"If I need to get away while I'm on shift and not get docked for taking an official break, there is a cut-out in the rear corridor. It has a very comfy chair and some television access, and it's free of security cameras, too. It's just that getting to it is the problem. It is **just** past the management office, just before the back exit.*

*... It is a risky endeavor, but I have sort of mastered it by now, and if anyone is paying any attention, which of course, they are **not**— they could rest assured to find me there, almost nightly. And once you*

reach it, it is smooth sailing. No one ever notices that corridor."

He remembers her discussing the timing of these distancing attempts as well, *"... I tend to spend my time there around 8:15, give or take, because Sean and Pat are still out of the office just after the dinner rush, but if I wait until 30 to get there, it is damn near impossible."*

Dylan hurriedly checked the time on his flip phone. It read 8:03 pm.

Now is your chance, dude! Channel Uncle Mike's hardcore green beret shit!

*Well, not the pressure points or anything, **no hand-to-hand**, just that sneaky co-op shit!*

Yes, it's a brilliant plan. He looked back over by the entrance. No Dozer.

We're all clear.

Move.

Dylan then grabbed a drink menu and held it up in front of his face as he moved briskly, yet casually, toward the hall between the public restroom area and the kitchen.

There, it must be. Through the kitchen.

Dylan maneuvered hastily, yet somehow still casually, to the impasse of the kitchen entryway and the floral atrium by the main barroom. He stopped before sliding through the doorway to the kitchen, as his heart raced incessantly.

This has to happen.

He saw through the diamond-shaped window on the door that there were two gentlemen of the waitstaff carrying trays of appetizers with them and heading for the exit from the kitchen. Dylan stepped to the side of the door, out of their line of sight, and awaited their triumphant escape. The two made their way through the doorway, with no notice or acknowledgment of Dylan's presence. Dylan then stealthily spun against the wall and into the path of the closing kitchen door. He was inside. He took a cursory glance at the layout of the kitchen. It closely resembled the layout of the food court kitchen at Temple. He raced into action before fear could overtake him and cause him to abort this mission.

He grabbed a white kitchen apron and overcoat ensemble that was lying in a pile on one of the heavy steel prep tables in the kitchen of the Goose. The attire was tossed asunder, probably from some disenfranchised worker who had his or her fill of the Goose for one day. As he dressed in the kitchen worker garb, he noticed a familiar smell. It enthralled him like he had never had an article of haphazardly discarded workwear do before. It smelled of cherry blossoms and apple orchards, or sweet fuchsias.

Jackie!

Dylan **knew** it was her. He rushed toward what appeared to be the back area of the kitchen. He looked over to his right as he passed an opening and saw a dishwashing machine for trays and kitchenware. He remembered it well from Temple.

Dishwasher! Yes!

*... if **that** is the dishwasher, **then**...*

He passed that opening, and looked to his left.

...Office!

He knew he was close, and his excitement rushed through him. He felt so alive in that moment.

This is what life must be like for some people!

He reached the now-famed cut-out with the television and comfy sofa. The corridor-type structure was dimly-lit. Dylan could see that there was a woman sitting on the chair in the far end of the embankment . He did his best to judge the woman's appearance.

Is it Jackie?

He knew that he had to be sure it was her before doing anything brash. Like running over to her.

Or kissing her.

Or drawing **any** attention to his existence in the back of their eating and drinking establishment.

*She's about her **height**...*

*She's has her hair **style**...*

*And **color**...*

And the room smells of her!

"**Jackie?**" he called out to her in his sweetest, most endearing voice.

*This could be the greatest moment of your entire life, dude! You **did** it!*

As the woman began to turn her head to look at Dylan, before he could even see her beautiful eyes gaze upon him, Dylan heard another familiar voice.

"**You again**?" Charles the bouncer had found his way back to the secret haven of doom. Well, it had to be doom now.

Before he could even gather his thoughts, Dylan was pushed against the wall, and with a resounding thud, he went down into a heap. Charles then grabbed Dylan and did things with him that he had only heard stories about or seen on the latest episode of OZ. Dylan was battered that day, en route to his forcible removal from the Goose.

Outside of the Goose, Dylan did perhaps the **dumbest** thing he had **ever** done before in his life. He broke away from Charles, and ran back into the Goose. He darted, almost heroically, against all odds, like he was Phil Collins or some shit, into the kitchen and back to the cut-off area by the back office. The woman was gone. He knew he had very little time to investigate, as Charles had given chase, despite Dylan's obvious speed and agility advantage over him. Dylan then began asking workers who had amassed in the kitchen, likely to bear witness to a disaster. Kinda like that gaper delay that you just **know** is going to ruin your morning commute, but you simply must take part in witnessing the distress.

Fucking humans.

"**Where is she?**" he shouted as the kitchen staff looked on helplessly and hopelessly. "Come on! I came from **Philadelphia! Phil-a-del-phia!** She was back here! This—" he said as he began to remove the kitchen attire that still adorned him, "is her outfit! She took it off! It smells like her hair!"

*This is what **crazy** must look like to **common folk**.*

"It smells like fuchsias! **It smells like fuchsias!**"

Crazy...

"I came from **Philly**!" Dylan broke down in frustrated tears, the blood from his lip slightly slurring his attempts to reason with these assholes. "**I love this girl!**"

Just then, Charles was there, pushing his way through the wait staff, who were mostly eager to comply with his desire to take down the perp. Charles reared back his fist an unloaded a furious haymaker that landed flush against Dylan's jaw. Dylan then collapsed into yet another uncomfortable heap. As he made his retreat from consciousness, he thought but one thing.

Jackie? Where'd you go?

Chapter Seven: Christine, Or Alicia, Or Smurfette

"You get one phone call, sir. You also have the right to legal representation, as you are set for a phone conference with Judge Berkshire-Smith in the morning. Your rights and your status will be discussed with you at, but **not until,** that time. Do you understand what I am saying to you?"

"I do."

I guess now is the time.

Dylan was escorted to what appeared to be a conference room, and he was presented with a rotary telephone. He dialed the number and waited.

The phone rang once.

The phone rang again.

*Please pick up! Please? **Please**?*

The phone rang a third time. This ring is shorter, and was interrupted by the sound of a click, followed by a breathy pause.

Then... "Hello? Dylan?? Is that you?!"

"Yes, it's me. I'm so sorry, dad! I am in Los Angeles again."

"What the **fuck** is wrong with you, boy?! **Where exactly** are you?" Sam said, with anger in his voice, but with obvious relief at hearing his youngest son was still alive.

"I got arrested tonight. I'm in holding here."

"Oh my God! **What** did you **do**, Dylan? **What did you do**?!"

"I came to make things right with Jackie. But I haven't found her yet, and her job had me arrested for sneaking around there looking for her."

"**Jesus Christ, boy**! You're an **ass**! When are... what is..." Sam was clearly frustrated by the situation, that was for sure. The officer in the conference room gestured toward his watch, as if to tell Dylan to pick up the pace of the conversation.

Dylan then interrupted his father. "Look, dad, I don't have time right now. Is mom there?"

Sam got silent for a moment, and Dylan felt a sudden rush of panic grip him. Sam spoke up. "No," he said. "She went after you 8 and a half days ago. Kay kept your secret for a bit, but he came clean to her. And you *know* your mom. I tried to stop her. She punched me in the mouth, so I had to let her go."

"Oh my God! I'm **so** sorry dad! Did she have any idea of where to look for me?"

"Your friend Ryan told her the Golden Goose, but I don't know if she found it or not," he said, with real concern in his voice. "I haven't heard from her in 5 days, and I just keep hoping that you'll both come back home in one piece."

"I'm **so sorry,** dad!"

"You just better hope your mom is okay, son! We both deserve better from you," Sam said, as he quickly pivoted his tone back to that of a concerned father. "When do you go before the magistrate?"

"In the morning. I don't have a lawyer. I'm gonna do without one. I know enough from school."

"**Please** get a public defender, boy! They are gonna chew you up there if you go in cocky. Please listen to me, for **once** in your life?"

"I gotta go, pop. I love you. And I'm sorry."

"Okay. If they ROR you, just come back home. Right away."

But Jackie.

Dylan knew better than to do anything else but cave and be fully complicit with everything his father was saying right then. Also, the officer seemed to be running short of patience with Dylan at that moment. He said his goodbyes and hung up the phone. After he finished, the officer escorted Dylan to a 6x8 holding cell on the bottom floor of the county jailhouse. Dylan entered it and saw that there were two other gentlemen inside of it. They were both bigger than Dylan, which made Dylan feel very nervous. Though it helped that Dylan had the facial evidence of the one-sided altercation with the bouncer earlier. Dylan had seen enough movies to rest assured that these marks would make him appear to be a hardened criminal, which of course, he was not.

There was only one steel cot and one completely exposed toilet in the cell.

*Please don't need to shit?! Thank **God** I didn't eat that much today! **Please** don't let these other guys **shit in front of me?! Please?!***

The larger of the men was Carl. He resembled WWF's Mark Henry. He even sounded a bit like him too! Sadly, it was not actually the "World's Strongest Man." That would have been a cool story to bring home to Philly!

About an hour into Dylan's stay with Carl and Griff, Dylan's worst fear from earlier came true. Carl dropped his prison wardrobe pants and squatted on the steel bowl in the center of the cell, and took one of the loudest, smelliest shits Dylan had ever even imagined. The smell of Carl's bowel decision ruined the remainder of the night, as Dylan struggled to breathe into the wee hours of the morning. Carl occupied the metal cot, selfishly alone. Griff was curled in a thin prison blanket in the corner of the cell. Dylan did the same, just in the opposite corner.

Truth is, Dylan only shut his eyes for what had to be 35 minutes.

I will not be Carl or Griff's bitch tonight!

***This asshole** will stay a **virgin asshole**!*

You hear me, you degenerate thugs!

No tight asshole for you!

Thankfully, the night went without incident, and in the morning, Dylan had his conference with Judge Reginald Berkshire-Smith. Luckily, the judge who was responsible for his fate must have gotten good head or something earlier in the morning, because he went very easy on Dylan. Dylan was released of his own recognizance. He was mainly able to do this by swearing that he would never even **consider** returning to the Golden Goose while still in LA, and that he would be leaving to go back to Philly in a few days.

Dylan left the county lock-up at almost 9 am. Thanks to the deal he made with the judge, he knew that the Golden Goose was no longer a viable option for him on his quest to reconnect with Jackie. As far as the judge was concerned, that quest was over. Dylan still held out hope that he would see her again and that this would all be set right. He then thought about Midge and her own insane quest to bring him back home safely, and he wondered where his forty-nine-year-old mother could be right now.

Now, he knew that forty-nine was not by any means old. But it wasn't vibrant and young either. And Midge had never really been outside of the tri-state area back east (Pennsylvania, New Jersey and Delaware). He knew that she likely would not have flown, especially given how unhappy Sam was with her decision to chase her irresponsible, lovesick son across the country. He also highly doubted that Midge would walk any further than a few blocks from their home back on Parrish Street. But he also knew he couldn't logically doubt just how far that woman might go for her kids. She really was an amazing mother. In this moment, in LA, Dylan hated her for it.

He walked to find a McDonald's. He knew that he could completely **destroy** a sausage egg and cheese McGriddle right about now. Before long, he did. While he sat in the McDonald's on La Brea Avenue, he made a rudimentary plan of action for the day. How could he find Jackie without access to the Goose?

Think, Dylan! What else had Jackie said about her daily existence in Hollywood?

He thought long and hard. He thought back to their third day together in LA. She had opened up quite a bit then.

Let's see...

"It isn't all you might expect it to be living here. When I'm not at the Goose, I'm generally more of a homebody. I live in an apartment complex on North Vista just north of Franklin. I rarely do much of anything. Just work and sleep, basically."

Thinking about that conversation didn't give him much of a plan of action, except but to hang out in the area North of Franklin. After his deliciously unhealthy breakfast, he made his way to N. Vista Street. When there, he saw very few spots to really go incognito or whatever. It was a very quiet, residential setting. It was unassuming and peaceful. He spent almost two hours there, just sort of pacing back and forth. There were families. There were children. There were border collies *aplenty*. But there was **no Jackie**.

What else did she say?

"On rare occasion, I might head to the Hollywood Bowl. Mainly that is just for concerts or whatever though."

Dylan looked in a neighborhood newspaper that he had taken from one of those bins on La Brea earlier. He scoured the event pages, and found the listing for the Hollywood Bowl. Much to his dismay, there were no concerts scheduled there for that day.

Back to the drawing board.

He knew that his only viable option at this point was the forbidden Goose. The thought of Charles reigning furious blows down upon him made his soul hurt. But what else could he possibly do?

You could just go home.

He then thought of his mother's journey.

It would all be for naught if you quit now, dude!

He then looked at his phone. It is such a simple option.

Why not?

The phone rang.

It rang again.

It rang a third time.

It then rang again, only to be cut short by a click.

"Jackie?!"

After a pause, her angelic voice began.

Look at you you're just as blind

Trying to grab your little piece of mind

And you want to hold it near

But you know you can't keep it

Say a little should suffice

But more than a little of you is so nice

And you give me what I want

Not when I need it

Not when I need it

Well I find it all the time,

But not when I need it.

Dylan was **so** excited to hear a new Matthew Sweet song sung by Jackie in this voicemail message. That means that she recently recorded a new message!

*She **does** still exist!*

She is alive!

After the beep, Dylan sprung into his response message with enthusiasm.

"Hey, Jackie!" he eagerly called out to the world, almost choking on his own excitement.

"Where are you? I'm on your street right now!"

That is a very scary sentence.

"I hitchhiked across the country and I got ejected from the Goose yesterday. I spent the night in county. I can't go back to your work anymore..."

Even scarier sentence, Dylan, bring it home.

... Can you please call me back, Jackie?"

How could she not?

Hammer it home!

"Please, Jackie? I love you. Please call me soon!"

Glorious! She'll call you! Relax!

Dylan kept on pacing down the street, back and forth, trying so desperately to blend in. He kept looking at the windows of the apartment complex, nestled on a grassy knoll.

I guess...

He made up his mind and walked over to the building. He entered the front foyer. He then looked to his right at the wall of mailboxes. He saw that there were no first names, only first initials.

Look for the J's.
Look for the J's.

Wait! *She uses a fake name.*

Fuck!

He remembered from his attempt at Clarissa back at the Goose. He then remembered Christine Lakin.

Look for the C's.

Look for the C's.

Wait! *Al from Step By Step!*

Look for the A's.

Look for the A's.

Dylan amassed a list of possible apartments. There were 5 options in total. There were 3 'C' names, and there were 2 'A' names.

What the fuck can you do with this?!

How else can we find her?!

I know! I know!

She has to be one of these!

What if she's not? What then?

I haven't thought that far ahead, ok?!

He then saw that three of the names (1 'A' and 2 'C's) were on the third floor. The other 'A' was on the second floor, whereas the other 'C' was on the bottom floor.

Bottom, middle or top floor?

He decided on the top floor. He then made his way to the stairwell. He still had no plan of action for when he reached that floor. He had the options of apartment 300, 305 and 308. He stood in front of 300. He timidly raised his hand, and knocked lightly on the door. After about 20 seconds, the door creaked open. A beautiful young woman answered in a plaid sundress.

She was **not** Jackie.

She was also not Christine Lakin.

"Hello? Can I help you, sport?"

"I'm sorry, I think I have the wrong apartment," he said, dejectedly. "I'm sorry."

"No, problem, kip!"

Fucking Hollywood!

He then made his way a few doors down to 305. He knocked again. The door cracked open. It was a young man, probably in his twenties. He answered the door while scrolling on a Blackberry device, not paying attention to the visitor at the door, at all.

"**Yes**?" the young stand-in actor said, in a voice that rivaled Vincent Price from one of his early works.

"I'm sorry, man! Wrong apartment."

The guy looked up at Dylan and offered, "Well, who are you after?"

"My friend Jackie lives in this building...

...Well, maybe not Jackie...

....Maybe Christine.

...Maybe Alicia."

"Well, my good man, I am **none** of those people! Have you tried calling her?"

"Yes, I think she is screening her calls though or something?"

The young man suddenly seemed very put-off in that moment. "Screening to avoid **you**, pal?"

"No, not screening...

...not, uh...

I-I.....

...I'm sorry..."

Just then, Dylan noticed that the girl in the sunflower dress from 300 was craning her neck out of her apartment to bear witness to Dylan's failed attempt to connect with the love of his life. When she noticed that he had noticed her, she hurriedly returned her prying, ostrich-like head to her apartment. Dylan could hear the door slam shut. The padlock being turned hard rang out and bounced off of the hardwood floors and the light-floral patterned wallpaper of the hall. Dylan had a familiar feeling of dread deep in his belly.

He turned away from the Made-For-TV movie extra's apartment and made his quick escape to the stairwell. When he arrived there, he began descending the stairs, but stopped momentarily as he heard a light commotion coming from the door to the bottom floor. In an instant, he knew what the commotion was. Sally Sundress had alerted the authorities about Dylan's presence in their building.

Not again.

Dylan quickly bounded down the stairs. When he reached the bottom, the doorway cracked open as an

LAPD officer maneuvered his way through the door frame. Dylan offered little hesitation, as he slithered by and sped past the officer and raced out of the building. The officer followed suit, but remember, Dylan was blessed with blazing speed, so officer John McClane's efforts to keep pace with Dylan were futile at best.

Dylan reached the street and kept on sprinting into the distance. He knew now that he was out of options.

I should just go home.

...It was all for naught.

A wiser young man might admit defeat in that moment. Dylan was no such young man. On his way to the Los Angeles subway, he began to concoct a game plan to return to the Goose to find Jackie, or Christine, or Alicia, or Smurfette. Whoever she might actually be.

Chapter Eight: Oh My Fuck!

As Dylan approached the corner across from the entrance to the Golden Goose, he saw that Charles "Dozer" Hogan was standing at the front door. It was only 6 pm. Dylan then recalled a conversation with his old friend.

*"My shift starts at 6:30, and I am never, ever, **ever** early. It's bad enough that I need to be there **for** my shift. I would rather do **anything else in the world** but be there even a minute longer than my paycheck requires me to be."*

In that same conversation, she'd also said, *"There is the back entrance to the place, of course. But I never enter through there. I like to get a sense of the main room when I get there. It prepares me for the type of night I expect to have. Those are the A-B-C's of my employment at the Golden Goose!"*

***God**, I miss her!*

Dylan was confident that he would not have to wait long to see Jackie arrive through the main doors. Now he simply needed to stay out of Charles' line of sight, and thus off of his radar.

Dylan sat on a step that was not directly across from the Goose. It was still close enough to clearly see the entranceway, just not in the direct path of where Dozer stood—as he was pivoted away from Dylan's vantage point. Dylan had a fool-proof plan for the off-chance that Dozer actually did look his way. Dylan has an LA Times opened up, and was vigilant and cunning enough to raise it into place should he need to.

Dylan was sure that Jackie would be working tonight. She always worked on Saturdays. He then worried because he had been sitting for a long time, and there was no sign of Jackie. He looked at his phone. The clock read 6:28 pm. Two minutes left until her shift begins. Just then he looked up at the entrance to the Goose. He sees Dozer talking to someone who appears to have just entered the building. Dylan can only make out maybe a shoulder from the opening of the door, and a bit of the person's hair.

Jackie?

 Dylan panicked. He knew that it **had** to be Jackie, and if he could just talk to her, she would keep Charles away from him. But, getting **to** Jackie would be the hurdle to overcome on this particular evening. Dylan would need to pick his spots.

Everybody goes to the bathroom sometimes.

It would be risky as hell to do. Dylan knew that if he got caught by Dozer again, not only would there be blood, but Dylan would face serious jail time. Like, **serious**. He remembered the deal he struck with Berkshire-Smith early that morning. Dylan would be just another prisoner guarded by men like his father back home. The thought, justifiably, scared Dylan immensely. Was it enough to make Dylan begin his trip back to Philly?

The obvious answer to that inquiry came when Dylan noticed that Charles seemed to be doing the "pee-pee" dance in his strong stance at the door. Truth be told, seeing such a large, angry, physically intimidating black man giving in to the urge to dance away his need to urinate made Dylan chuckle. It was **adorable** to witness, and Dylan felt fortunate to have beheld it on this evening. Once Charles made his way fully inside, likely to go to the restroom to relieve his urge, Dylan sprang into action. He slithered into the club, and as he had expected it to be, it was already very full of customers. Dylan would use this state to assist him in blending in. He even headed to the bar at one point. He was hoping that Jackie would be tending the main bar, as she commonly had done. Much to his chagrin, a man named Kent was tending the bar this evening.

"Hey! Can I get you someth—"

What? The fuck?!

Kent was one of the observers involved in the "gaper-delay" situation in the kitchen the previous night. Dylan panicked, because he recognized Kent from when he questioned the staff about Jackie's whereabouts. You know? When he removed the kitchen attire and spewed utter nonsense at them, before Dozer performed his best Riddick Bowe right hook to Dylan's jawline?

Kent continued in a bit of a panic, "do they kn— ... are you—"

Get to the point Kent Tekulve!

"You're not allowed **in here**! I'm gonna get my—"

Dylan spoke up, quickly, in an attempt to ease Kent's worried, troubled mind. "I know, man. I know. I'm not trying anything. At all. I don't want any trouble. I'm just trying to get a beer and a bourbon. That's all."

Kent had relaxed his tense demeanor, and began getting Dylan's drink order together. He then spoke up,

"Yeah, I got it man. We have Flying Fish, domestic drafts, and malternatives."

"Flying Fish is great. Thanks! And a shot of Beam."

Kent returned with the beverages and inquired, "So, you got your **ass kicked** yesterday. What were you spouting about in the kitchen?"

"My friend Jackie works here, but she told me she gave you guys a fake name when she started here. So I'm struggling to find her. I'm from Philly, actually. She came there to visit me, but she left under bad circumstances, so I just had to make things right. You know? I gotta find her, man!"

Kent seemed very sympathetic to Dylan's plight. He did his best to reason with him. "Wow, I'm sorry to hear that, man! I started here two weeks ago, so I don't really know many people here. My sister Clarissa works the event room and got me the gig."

Ah, I know her!

"That's cool, man."

"And look, man. You just gotta understand about yesterday, people are losing their shit cause of terrorism now. 9/11 fucked everything all up. So, Chuck had to bounce you like that, man! I swear, he's a good dude!"

*Yeah, he seems like a real **peach**! My favorite!*

"I know, man. I wanna thank you for being so cool about this stuff, pal. So, you don't know if my friend is working tonight?"

"No, man. Again, I don't really know people here. I know I took over for someone who was a long-timer here. But I dunno anything about them. I don't even know if they were a boy or a girl."

Kent put a thought into Dylan's head.

Maybe Jackie finally worked up the courage to give up the gig she hates?

Maybe she is going back to school!

I told her she should do that! ***Me!***

Maybe she listened!

When Dylan thought this, he was flooded with emotions. All at once.

I'm scared I might never see her again.

I'm so proud of her for going back to school to better her situation.

*I'm **such** a good friend for advising her to do that.*

*A **great friend**, even.*

Dylan finished his drinks as Kent returned to his task of bartending. He then came back, quickly, and leaned over to Dylan, almost like he wanted to share something privately with him.

"What's up, man?" Dylan asked curiously. Kent leaned in and said, almost in a whisper, "Chuckie is heading this way, get out of here, man!"

Shit!

Fucking shit!

Dylan took out his wallet and struggled to get it open. As he did, Kent spoke up quietly again, "Just **go**, man! I got this!"

Good people do still exist.

"**Yo!**" Charles shouted as Dylan made his quick escape through the crowd. He then circled back to get to and through the door, never to encounter Charles again. As he walked on Hollywood Boulevard, he noticed that his phone's red light was on. A notification symbol.

Perhaps a missed call? A voicemail? He got very excited.

Jackie?!

With great enthusiasm he flipped open his phone to see that he had indeed missed several calls, and did have a voicemail. He pushed '1,' hit the call button and listened.

"Two messages. First new message."

Much to his chagrin...

"Yeah, Dylan? It's Sammie. I don't even know if you are getting this or not, but we need you home ASAP. Dad just had to drive to West Virginia to pick up mom. She walked to try to get to you, and she wound up at a mountain pass in West Virginia. The Dutton Gap, I think? She had to stop to use a phone at a mountain home. She was attacked." There was a bit of a pause, then he continued. "She's ok," Sammie said, with a slight pause. "The guy is not. She's **freaking** out now. They gotta, (indiscernible)."

The voicemail cut off.

"New message."

"Um, okay... where was I? Yeah, she hit him with a goddamned table leg. Broke his nose and busted his skull. She's in a police station. Dad is heading there. He said he has to figure out the best course of action going forward. I have **never** seen Dad this mad before. He's talking about jail time, dude. **Mom! In jail!** He's gonna see who he can talk to or whatever. You really **fucked** things up this time, Dylan. Give me a call as soon as you get this."

Dylan hung up the phone. He had no idea what he could possibly do now. He never expected his mother to actually try to walk to California. Even **he** couldn't do it, as athletic and young as he was. Midge was neither young **nor** athletic. Midge showed Dylan that nothing would get in her way if she thought her son was in danger. In that moment, he felt honored to have her as a mother.

How can I ever face them again?

*Because of me, my mother is probably facing assault charges, and perhaps West Virginia law will now dictate that **table legs** are considered **deadly weapons**!*

And dad has never hit me before. He probably hits like Dozer. But with dad's Italian anger.

*Oh my **fuck**!*

Chapter Nine: Tomorrow, and tomorrow, and tomorrow

Dylan nestled upon his new bed at the park on Lexington. He had no idea what his next move would be. He could never bring himself to face Midge or Sam again, though he somehow knew they would eventually forgive him. They always did. But maybe this time was a "bridge too far."

A bridge...

too far.

He then heard a hauntingly familiar voice.

*"You got it **now**.*
*Maybe **this** is what you were **meant** to do.*

*Be **here**.*

***Now**.*

*For **it**."*

Dylan couldn't keep to himself about it, as he shouted back at the voice, "What the **fuck** are you talking about? I was **meant** to do what?"

The voice was in an explanatory sort of mood tonight, as it continued. *"I think you **know**. It is **your** destiny. What you **should** have done on **Girard**. But this is more romantic. **Cali** suits you. It's what **you** were made for."*

Dylan then shouted into the darkness, "**Just go**! **I'm good**."

Just then, from the darkness at the park on Lexington, there crept a small, shadowy figure. As it approached Dylan, he could see that it was an older, disheveled man in a tattered army jacket and oil-stained jean shorts that were cut off just below his knees. He wore a pair of black leather standard-issue military boots. He went by "Sambo."

As he approached, he addressed Dylan in a stern, yet helpful tone. "You okay, buddy? Anything I can help you with?" Dylan could only think of one thing in that moment. He dejectedly said, "I just don't want to be here anymore."

Sambo then quickly retorted in agreement, "I hear ya there! None of us do!"

Sambo then made a recommendation that Dylan could really hatch his wagon to. "Have you ever heard of the Colorado Street Bridge?" Sambo asked with a sort of hope in his voice. "It is a very **helpful** spot. I lost four friends there in the last year and a half. It's in Pasadena, about 11 miles away from here."

Dylan said nothing. There was nothing to say. He simply gathered his things. As he did, it dawned on him that he didn't need his things where he was going. Well, he needed one thing.

He picked up his discman and loaded a new mixed CD. He left his satchel behind. There was only one song he wanted to hear right now. He cranked it way up, turned silently and purposefully away from Sambo and walked on.

> *Life it seems to fade away*
> *Drifting further every day*
> *Getting lost within myself*
> *Nothing matters no one else*
> *I have lost the will to live*
> *Simply nothing more to give*
> *There is nothing more for me*
> *Need the end to set me free*

Dylan had found his way to Bronson Avenue. He had heard about this bridge a few years back, so he had a rough idea of its location in relation to him now. He kept on, with anxious purpose.

Things not what they used to be

Missing one inside of me

Deathly loss this can't be real

Cannot stand this hell I feel

Emptiness is filling me

To the point of agony

Growing darkness taking dawn

I was me but now, he's gone

He had found his way to Fountain Avenue. He thought about the moment on Girard the night Jackie left his life. If only she had answered any of his calls. If only he had paid attention to the numerous obvious signs that she was falling for him. If only he didn't get head from Jessica.

No one but me can save myself, but it's too late
Now I can't think, think why I should even try
Yesterday, it seems as though it never existed
Death greets me warm, now I will just say goodbye

Goodbye...

During the epic, heartbreaking guitar solo, Dylan walked very briskly along Fountain Avenue. He set the song to repeat for the next almost 4 hours. He listened to that destructively beautiful anthem over and over again. He had never been this confident in a decision before. Yet, there were still many things that he struggled with as he walked to his final resting place. There were so many things and people he would miss badly. The main person he thought of was his mother. God, he loved that woman. But he knew how badly he probably had hurt her by jumping ship on his life back home to chase the dream of a forever love with Lara...

...*With* ***Jackie!***

....Yes. With **Jackie**.

*I miss **Jackie**.*

I'll miss dad.

I'll miss Kay.

I'll miss Calvin.

I'll miss Sammie.

I'll miss Ryan.

I'll miss Steve.

*What the **fuck** are you talking about, dude?! You won't **miss anyone**! That's the whole point of this!*

***This** is your destiny!*

                       ***This** is your fate!*

***This** is probably the greatest gift that Jackie could have given to you.*

                       *... **She is your way out!***

The Colorado Street Bridge is one of the most infamous spots in the country for people committing suicide. So many people had done the deed there in the 20th century that the bridge was commonly referred to as "Suicide Bridge" in popular culture. Dylan was confident he was following a correct path. He found his way to a capstone on the main thoroughfare. He used his agile body to hoist himself upward onto the ledge facing the divide below.

This is it.

Your destiny.

Your fate.

.

Your purpose.

Your moment of reverence.

After the solo to Fade To Black ended for probably the 30th or 31st time, he decided a change of pace was in order for this pinnacle moment of his journey. He flipped ahead three tracks on his mixed CD to the new perfect song.

A long December,
And there's reason to believe
Maybe this year will be better than the last
I can't remember the last thing that you said as
you were leavin'
Now the days go by so fast

"... Remember that New Year's Eve that you and the boys sang this for Midge? That was a great moment!"

And it's one more day up in the canyons

And it's one more night in Hollywood

If you think that I could be forgiven

I wish you would

"... I don't ever deserve forgiveness for letting you suffer, Mom. Your life would have been better without me. I can fix that now."

The smell of hospitals in winter

And the feeling that it's all a lot of oysters,

but no pearls

All at once you look across a crowded room

To see the way that light attaches to a girl

And it's one more day up in the canyons

And it's one more night in Hollywood

If you think you might come to California

I think you should...

"... I did everything I was gonna do with this shit life. It is all behind me. Only downhill from here..."

Drove up to Hillside Manor

Sometime after two a.m.

And talked a little while about the year

I guess the winter makes you laugh

a little slower,

Makes you talk a little lower

about the things you could not show her

And it's been a long December,

and there's reason to believe

Maybe this year will be better than the last

I can't remember all the times

I tried to tell myself

To hold on to these moments as they pass.

*...**What** is this gonna do to Mom? And Dad? They don't need to hear about you on some nightly news broadcast, or worse yet, just a phone call from some detective...*

> *And it's one more day up in the canyon*
> *And it's one more night in Hollywood*
> *It's been so long since I've seen the ocean*
> *I guess I should*

Dylan then spoke defiantly, as he stood overlooking his final resting place. "This isn't for **me**. I'm **better** than this." As he stepped off of that ledge, he suddenly felt like he had a new lease on life. Yes, he would have a whole lot of mess to clean up in his life now. What is he gonna do? Can he go home? He knew that if he didn't make a drastic change back home, he would just end up here, or worse, all over again. It was then that he decided, with a heavy heart, that he wouldn't return home again. He would put his nose to the grindstone and make something of himself, on his own, out in California. He made his way back toward Hollywood. After all, he felt like he kinda knew his way around there, at least a bit by now. So he felt a little bit better off there.

He returned to the bench on Lexington to find it was occupied by a homeless woman who was foraging through his satchel, which he had left on the bench while he was in his dismay earlier in the evening.

Remember mom's lesson from when you were five...
About how to deal with strangers in a strange place...

Come in loony!

Dylan charged toward the bench, spouting the most illogical nonsense imaginable. As he waved his arms up over his head, he shouted, "Richard Nixon swam in the Chartreuse Lagoon with Marilyn Monroe! They ate snacks and played tiddlywinks!

They played Tiddlywinks!!"

The woman looked as if she had seen six ghosts riding in a van, listening to the Grateful Dead. She ran away from the park, though she did make off with a pair of Dylan's clean boxers, and one pair of tube socks.

Damn her to hell!

Not the tubes!

Dylan pulled out his phone and placed a dreaded phone call. It only rang maybe a half a time, then he heard that horrid click. "Hello? Dylan?"

Gulp.

The time had come.

The time had come.

"Yeah, hi mom!"

Her voice did not seem angry. Shockingly, it just sounded relieved. Like Dylan's voice was the greatest sound her ears had ever heard before. She began to cry. "Oh my God, baby!" She choked out, "Where **are** you??"

...Big Gulp.

"I'm so sorry, mom! I'm on a park bench in West Hollywood. I didn't find Jackie."

 Midge sounded like her good feeling had all but run out. "**Look**, Dylan. You **need** to come home. We will wire you money to catch a plane, just be careful! You scared me **so** bad!"

...Double Gulp...

 He limped into his next statement, "Look, mom, I know I scared you. I know I messed up... and I'm sorry.

...But I'm gonna stay here."

"The **fuck** you are, boy! Get to a Western Union **right now** and call us when you're there!"

After several failed attempts to get a word in edgewise to his mother, Dylan broke the fourth wall. "I almost **killed myself** tonight, mom."

There was a long, somber pause, as though Midge was struggling to find the right words to say in such a volatile moment. She then spoke up, in her most soothing voice possible. "**What**, Dylan? What do you **mean**? **What happened?**"

Dylan could hear his father reacting in the background, seemingly unaware of exactly what Dylan had just said. Sam was likely only reacting to the inquiry of his wife. Dylan could hear the commotion in the background, complete with the jangle of Sam's keys being scooped up from the dining room table.

*Is he gonna **drive** to Hollywood?! Come on guys!*

Dylan then heard his mother pull away from the phone, as though she was in a physical struggle of sorts there. The sound of the jangling keys came to a halt, as Midge said, "Just wait! Please? Just wait, boob!"

She then returned her head to the phone. She spoke up, in a supportive, almost sympathetic tone. It was a tone that Dylan couldn't remember ever hearing from his tough-as-nails mother before. She said, "I know, boy. I know."

"What do you mean, mom?"

"I know what you are feeling. I want you to stay there. Just be careful. And **please** don't avoid us... We love you here. You are **very** loved.

...I would gladly give up my life for you right now if God asked me to. **You know that**, don't you?"

*What kind of God is gonna bring that kind of request to a **mother of four**?? For shame, God! **For shame!***

"I know, mom! I know! I'm gonna be ok. I promise!" Dylan hated lying to his mother like that. But what else could he do? He then continued, "I love you mom! And I'm sorry about everything! I'm sorry about the guy too!"

Dylan decided to approach the delicate matter of the assault charge, "A **table leg**? Really, mom? A **table leg**?"

"I stopped and asked to use a phone to call your dad, 'cause there was a mountain lion in the woods." She paused, and then continued. "...And you know how I feel about cats!"

*Amazing. Simply **amazing**.*

Midge continued telling the story of the table leg to the dome. "And this guy **took out his peppy**, so I turned to leave. I would rather get eaten by a cougar then deal with that. He grabbed my shoulder, so I punched him. He took me down, I reached around for what I could find, and I grabbed the leg to his end table. It broke off so I clocked him with it. The first one got him off of me, the second one was his nose, the third one was his head. Then I started banging his head into the floor."

"Oh God, **you psycho**! I think that was probably excessive, but good job, mom! Can I talk to Dad?"

"I really don't think it's smart right now. He's j—..." The sound of a struggle was evident and then stopped abruptly. "...Yeah? **Dylan**?! What the **fuck** is your problem, **boy**?!"

Dylan didn't know how to handle this relationship dynamic. It was always dad who was soft-spoken and mom who was authoritative.

*What the **shit** is this?*

"I'm sorry, dad! I just had t—..."

"I don't want to hear it, I'm sending you 200 dollars to a Western Union, and you're coming back home tonight! **Understood**?"

"Dad, I d—..." Just then there was the sound of another struggle as Midge took the phone back.

"You know where I stand. Be safe, Dylan. We love you. Don't worry about dad. He will call you when he calms down."

"Okay, I'll talk to you soon, mom!"

There was a long pause. Midge then reluctantly spoke up, with a sort of sigh that worried Dylan to hear.

"I'm not gonna be here for a bit. I'll be fine, boob. Stay in touch with your brothers and your dad. I love you, Dylan. To the moon, and back!"

"Mom? What do you **mean** you won't be here?"

"I'm fine. I gotta go to the hospital for a bit. I'm fine. Don't worry. It is getting taken care of! I'll be okay! I love you!"

*Is my mom **dying**? Is it because of **me**?*

"I love you too, mommy! Please be well!"

"Bye Dylan! Goodnight." The phone call ended, and Dylan felt both better **and** worse all at the same time. He felt a great relief that he spoke to his mom again after the Thomas "Table Leg To The" Crown Affair in West Virginia, but he was now worried that he may have caused his mother's untimely demise through his selfish actions. As he closed his eyes to sleep on that cold steel park bench in his last remaining pair of dirty undies, he could only seem to think of one thing.

Tomorrow...

... And tomorrow.

.
A
n
d

t
o
m
o
r
r
o
w

.

Chapter Ten: ...Hello?

"I'm playing at the 901. I go on at 8:30. I've done solo sets the last three years or so. But my stuff is really full band material. I just need to find band mates for the shows."

"When does your shift end? Can I take you out for a latte?"

"**Absolutely**. I get off at 4:30. But this is just a hold-over gig, man. I'm friends with the manager. I can bounce anytime, really."

Dylan was excited at the idea of getting a latte with Gerald Dunphy. Gerald used to work for EMI records in the '90's, at the time when they signed Vladimir John Ondrasik II, and encouraged him to change his name. He became "Five For Fighting" and then blew up as a huge success in 2001. That isn't to say that Gerald was directly responsible for Five For

Fighting's stardom in the late 90's, but who knows? Though EMI since had disbanded as a company, Gerald retained his status as a local legendary talent scout. He now shifted his focus to discovering indie rock performers with character, which he said that Dylan absolutely was.

"Give me a few minutes to work my magic on Tomas, and I should be out front in a jiff. Ok, Gerald?"

"Yes, sounds good, sport! You can call me Jerry!"

"K, Jerry, I'll be right with you!"

Gerald waited out front. After he worked his magic on Tomas, Dylan pushed open the front door of the McDonald's in Encino. Dylan had the keys to his blue-on-blue PT Cruiser. It was a dick-head car, but it was roomy enough for his equipment, and got ok gas-mileage, or so it seemed.

Dylan was dressed in his attire for the gig tonight, and he had his acoustic with him. Dylan bought this Taylor acoustic/electric with money from his financial aid package two years before. Dylan had been a USC Trojan for much of the last 3 years. His credits from his Freshman year at Temple transferred over, though it was a big hassle to do so. He carried his guitar with him almost everywhere he went.

He decided to establish a place for himself in his new life in the LA area. He now had an apartment. He lived in the complex where Jackie had said she lived. Though he kept his heart open for her return, he had yet to see her again.

"We can head to my favorite spot in Burbank, would that be ok?" Gerald asks Dylan. "Unless you wanted to get to the gig much earlier."

"No, that'd be fine. I can take us there now. I haven't had a good latte in a dog's age, man!"

"You're so fuckin' cool!" Gerald said, pumping rainbows up Dylan's asshole.

"Thanks, pal," Dylan said, trying to act as aloof as he could in that moment. "I do what I do."

"I can get my assistant to get me from the place after we finish."

As they got in the car and Dylan was positioning his guitar in the backseat, Gerald pivoted his attention to the elephant in the car. "So, you carry your guitar **everywhere** with you? To McDonalds? Where you work?"

Dylan knew he would need to address this at some point, so why not now? "You never know when inspiration is gonna strike. It is the worst when it does and you gotta wait three hours before you can write a song. By then, it's gone. And you're fucked!"

Gerald seemed blown away. "So, do you write a lot of your songs like that? Just **wherever** you are in the world, at a given time, *when the inspiration hits you?*"

"Music is an amazing thing, man! Whoever **it** is out there that wants me to craft these tales, **they** put the idea in my head at **their** leisure," Dylan said, with Bob Dylan, or whoever's words seemingly falling from his lips right now. "I just **gotta** be a receptive muse, and do my part."

"Wow, man!" Jerry said, smiling. "Just **wow!**"

They reached Mrs. Bean, the hip, trendy, yet somehow unassuming café and noshery in Burbank. Dylan held open both the car door, **and** the front door for Gerald, which surprised him. He genuinely was not used to a prospective client with manners like that, especially not in the Los Angeles area. The two stood at the counter, and when it was their turn, Dylan attempted to speak up, when Gerald interjected over Dylan's voice.

"Yes, hello, miss. Can you get us two venti lavender lattes?" he said with authority, then continued, "**As is?**"

Dylan then spoke up, from the rear. "Can I have mine iced?" He then noticed that Gerald had some sort of look on his face, to which Dylan added for clarity, "I think it's just too hot for a hot drink today."

Gerald then laughed, and gestured with his thumb toward Dylan, "This guy! **This** guy! **Am I right?**"

Dylan laughed nervously, as though he had just blown his shot at being signed by Gerald Dunphy Productions, or "GDP," to which they are commonly referred. As they sat, and Jerry complimented Dylan's request at the counter, Dylan felt confident that he had not blown his chances with GDP.

"You know something? I do this **quite** a bit, and **no one** has had the guts to personalize their order **after** I placed it at the counter. I respect those **balls** you got, kid."

"I don't really know about my 'balls', sir, I just know what I like, and my dad raised us to not waste someone else's money. If you ordered me a drink that I didn't want, it'd be a waste of your hard-earned money, and that just **can't** happen."

Gerald was impressed. "Your dad sounds like he has a good head on his shoulders! My kind of man."

"Yeah, he's pretty awesome! I gotta call him after we get finished and before the show, he wanted an update about it."

Gerald smiled, "Does he *know* we are meeting? Does he know **me**?"

"**Everyone** knows you, Jerry," Dylan said confidently. "And yes, I told him we were meeting."

"Well, Dylan, I want you to call him and tell him that I am offering you a contract with me, given how the crowd receives you tonight, of course."

Dylan couldn't help but smile as he heard this news. He quickly tried to cover his enthusiasm, so as not to appear too eager. It was another lesson taught to him by his father years ago.

"Oh, that's awesome, Jerry! Thank you," he said, before offering, "You have **nothing** to worry about with the crowd reaction. I **promise** you that!"

"The word on you is out, Dylan Stewart. I'm not worried about the crowd tonight at all! That's why I'm here right now. Well, you've never had representation before, right?"

"No. Never. Just me on my own."

"And you don't have any management help, anywhere? No roadies? Anything?"

"No. Again. It is just me."

"Ok, that's good. It'll make this an easier deal. It will likely be a two-record thing. You'd be brought in to try out members of your studio band for the recordings."

"Man, that'd be awesome! But can I just record the things that I do play? I got rhythm guitar, bass and drums. I also do the lead guitar on a few of the tracks, in studio. Really, I would just need help with some stuff, here and there. And to tour, of course."

"Sounds good, man. Sounds good. I'm gonna head back to the Santa Ana office to work out some contract stuff, then I'll be at the show for the opener."

Dylan stood up as Gerald made his exit. Then Dylan sat back down, brimming with excitement. He then pulled out his phone, and called home.

"Hello, Dylan? That you?"

"Yeah, dad, it's me!" Dylan said, "How is mom doing?"

"Let's not talk about that, boy. Did you get it?"

Let's not talk about that?? What does that mean?

Dylan continued. "Yes, dad. He said it will be a two-record deal if tonight goes well! So, this is kinda like a try-out, I guess!"

Sam sounded excited, but Dylan expected a bit more enthusiasm from his dad.

Mom must be having problems.

"Look, dad, if you want me there, I can head back home, the semester is over now. I have a 3.45 GPA. I can head back for a few weeks."

"If you come back now, I will break my foot off in your ass boy! You hear me? You stay there. Your mom is fine."

"Are the guys there with you?"

"Kay is in Perkasie now. He runs a complex there. Calvin and his wife are in Jersey now. Sammie is teaching up at Marywood. We're fine here. Don't worry."

"Dad?" Dylan said, trying to draw a line in the sand with his voice as best he could. "What is going on with mom? I won't perform tonight until I know."

"**God**, you're an ass!" Sam continued, "Okay, so she got discharged last month. The judge is letting her walk on the assault, because she made good progress at Halpern. Your mother is a strong woman, Dylan. She's stronger than I am."

"I know, Dad. She's awesome! Where is she now?"

"She's asleep. She's been sleeping a lot more now 'cause of the medicine. They upped her dose on everything," he said, before getting very serious with Dylan. "You should know, **she** made all of this happen.

She kept me from getting your ass home. **She** pushed you to be your own man."

"I know, dad. I know she did. I'm sorry I'm not there."

"Dylan, go kick that gig's ass tonight and get that contract. I'm proud of you. I want you to remember that no matter what happens, me and your mother will always be here for you. We will do whatever it takes for you, Dylan. I love you."

Something is amiss. For dad to be speaking so cryptically is a strange and new happening. And dropping the L bomb too?

Something is up.

But the gig.

The contract.

*The reason for **all** of this.*

"I love you too, dad! I'll check back in tomorrow."

"Ok, Dylan. Good luck! You got this! I'm so proud of you!"

"Dad, are you su—...

(Silence)

...Dad? Do you wa—...

(Utter silence)

...Hello? Hello?"

Sam had hung up, likely never to hear that Dylan attempted to continue the conversation.

Hello?

Chapter Eleven: This Cannot Be

The 901 Bar and Grill was filled to capacity. Turns out that Gerald Dunphy was totally right when he told Dylan that the "word was out on Dylan Stewart." It seemed as though the entire student body of USC was in attendance to see Dylan perform his acoustic set that evening. And Dylan surely was not going to disappoint them in his effort to earn a recording contract from GDP, which he knew was dependent upon the crowd reaction to his set tonight.

He knew that the crowd was likely there to hear a few of his songs more than the others, but he really didn't much like playing the songs that were inspired by Jackie, or even *Cerulean*, which he played **for** Jackie on the hood of her Camaro on Mulholland before. Though he really disliked the painful memories, he knew that the importance of tonight transcended his own bitter feelings. So he played *Cerulean* for them.

As it winded down to a conclusion, a moment he was not fully anticipating occurred.

... I will wash myself in Cerulean.

Maybe, someday

I'll come clean...

As the high reverb setting made the last open chord resonate and fade into the night, the crowd had broken into a slow and steady chant that rose from the back of the room to the front of the stage.

"Saaavior!

...Saaavior!"

Dylan had not totally prepared himself to perform that power ballad tonight. He wrote it a few nights after Jackie went back to LA. The memory of how he felt watching the red lights fade into the distance from the platform at 30th Street Station haunted him to this day.

Dylan recorded a full band version of it on his 4-track minidisc recorder that he had purchased from eBay. He had gotten the recordings onto cassette tapes, like it was the early 90's again. He then passed out copies of the recorded demo around campus in his sophomore year, and the song's heartfelt lyrics and hauntingly brooding vocals garnered much notoriety for him around USC as a singer/songwriter. As such, he knew in his heart of hearts that people would clamor to hear him perform a bare-boned rendition of it tonight.

He thought of what was riding on this performance, so he knew how he was going to play to the crowd. When the chanting filled the venue and the crowd was calling for the ballad in complete and total unison...

"Saaavior!

..Saaavior!

..Saaavior!"

... Dylan stopped and looked around. He did his best to build the anticipation, by staying totally still, with his fingers positioned accordingly on his fretboard. The chanting crowd brought their chanting to a halt, and the anticipation was rather palpable. Just then, Dylan began to slowly and deliberately pick the open C chord. The crowd exploded joyously and loudly as Dylan began playing the intro to *Savior*.

I walk around

To see my world

Crumble down.

I've lost my friend.

I've lost my love.

I've lost all will

To push or shove.

I've tried my best

To get it right

I've seen myself

Awake at night.

I toss and turn,

As tears roll down.

Please rescue me,

Tear these walls down.

You could save my life tonight,

With just one kiss, you could make things right.

I won't put up a fight, I'd let you win.

Open your arms, and let me in.

Dylan realized that the crowd had been singing every word along with him to that point. He then turned the microphone stand toward the crowd, as if to gesture that it was "on them" to provide the vocals now. The crowd erupted during the slight guitar break. They then sang, in complete and total unison.

I lie awake

In this city.

I think of you,

Hey, do ya think of me?

I need you here,

Right next to me.

But you're far away,

All the way across this sea.

If I had money, I'd fly to you.

I'd buy you the stars,

And I'd give you the moon.

All I can do now, is promise I'm here,

And I'm waiting for you to appear.

Dylan was completely blown away by the fact that the crowd hadn't missed a beat. They were singing **every single word**.

You could save my life tonight,

*With just one kiss, you could make **me** right.*

I won't put up a fight, I'd let you win.

Open your arms, just let me in

Dylan grabbed the microphone, turned it to himself and said to the crowd, "Good job guys! Here we go!"

I am lost,

> *And I need you*
>
> *To be my everything tonight.*
>
> *Save me from myself,*
>
> *I need a phone call tonight.*
>
> *I am lost, and I need you*
>
> *To be my everything in life.*
>
> *Save my from myself,*
>
> *I need a savior tonight.*

Dylan then stepped onto the distortion/reverb combo pedal. He played the guitar solo on his own, with no backing guitar, and the audience went absolutely bonkers. Then Dylan began to sing again.

> *I am lost,*
>
> *And I need you*
>
> *To be my everything tonight.*
>
> *Save me from myself,*

I need a phone call tonight.

I am lost, and I need you

To be my everything in life.

Save my from myself,

I need a savior,

A saaav-iorr!

To-nighht!

I need you! I neeed youu

Too-niight!

The crowd was going absolutely crazy, but there was a moment as Dylan was wailing high with his vocal screams, that the emotion of the moment overtook him. He was in tears. After the raucous ending of the song, he collected himself, as the crowd looked on with what appeared to be sincere concern for Dylan. He began a softer open chord section of the chorus, with much softer, almost speaking vocals.

> *I am losing*
>
> *Every moment*
>
> *Without you in my life.*
>
> *I need you every day*
>
> *I need you, Jackie.*

He stopped playing as the crowd was obviously affected by what they saw and heard. The uproarious applause that had accompanied his set that evening was gone from the room at that moment.

He couldn't even bring himself to raise his eyes to look at the crowd, and when he finally did, he could hardly see the faces of the audience through the reflection of the low lights that illuminated the spot where he stood on the stage. The lights reflected off of the tears in his eyes, and made it very difficult to connect with the audience, like he always prided himself on his ability to do.

Just then, he saw a girl heading for the exit from the back of the room. She was looking back over her shoulder as she made her escape.

He knew who it was.

"**Jackie?**" he shouted, as the crowd all eagerly turned their attention toward the back of the room. He threw off his Taylor to the floor behind him and jumped off the stage in a panic. He pushed his way through the "Stewart Collective" that was watching the show that night. As he made his way to the back door, he passed a table in the back where Gerald Dunphy sat with one of the radio DJ's of local KROQ in Los Angeles. As Dylan locked eyes with Gerald, he felt an immense pressure deep in his chest. He kept on out the door. He knew what he had to do.

He had found Jackie.

He thought of his mother's mental health decline, and the corresponding tension it was causing his father. He thought of his broken relationships back home with his dear friends and with his brothers, who were all but estranged from him now. They all blamed him for breaking apart their happy Parrish Street family and their "Pleasantville" existence. **He knew that** in his heart of hearts. He knew then that if he didn't make things right with Jackie, right now, that it was...

        ...all for naught.

        This cannot be.

Chapter Twelve: Daddy?

Dylan rushed out the door of the 901. He began calling out as he hustled along.

"Jackie?...

Jackie?

Come back?

Pleeeeaasse?!"

He searched and searched in every direction.

Much to his dismay, he saw no one.

How fast can she be??

He looked for her car. As he reached the street, he noticed a long blue sedan pulling into the distance. He looked at it as it drifted down Gayley Avenue.

This can't be happening!

Not again.

As he thought this, he stepped back on the side of Gayley. The audience had largely spilled out of the 901, many trying to see what happened to their star. Many of the crowd had approached closely to where Dylan was standing. But none of them had the guts to make contact with Dylan. That was probably for the best anyway. He hadn't even thought about what jumping off of stage after weeping like a tortured baby in the middle of his big show might have done to his career as a rising musical artist. As he stood there, with all of his adoring and confused fans at his back, he watched the red tail lights of what he was sure was Jackie's Camaro pulling off into the distance. Just then, for the first time in a few years now, his right hand began to shake at his side.

Jackie is gone.

Again.

I can't believe she came!

    Just then, he was rushed back into the moment. He was suddenly completely aware of his amassment of adoring fans at his rear. He knew that it was likely time for him to *face the music*.

    He slowly turned around in his stance to greet the audience. He put on his bravest smirk as he began to address the crowd.

"Sorry about that," he blurted out. "I thought I saw someone?"

One of the girls in the crowd, who was trooped by her girlfriends, shouted out in her most ditsy, flamboyantly irreverent tone, "Jackie??"

Her friends giggled and playfully smacked her shoulder, like they were trying to say, "**As if**?!"

Fucking tart!

"No," Dylan laughed uncomfortably. "I thought I saw an old chum... it wasn't her."

Dylan then continued on, in a forlorn tone of voice and demeanor, "I gotta get out of here, guys!"

The crowd let out an audible refusal of these terms. They weren't an angry mob. After all, this was an indie college bar gig. They were very, very, **very** disheartened. Dylan felt their pain, but he could not imagine being in the proper state or frame of mind with which to perform any longer tonight.

He returned to the stage to gather his guitar and equipment. He began the process of unplugging and packing it up. The crowd, which had all but returned to the pit in front of the stage, began to clamor for more Dylan Stewart. It started very low, in an almost monotonous manner.

"Dy-lan...

...Dylan..."

Over the next few minutes, the monotoned murmur of the crowd rose to a full-on roar.

"**Dylan!**

...**Dylan!**

...**Dylan!**"

...Dylan!!"

Dylan couldn't believe what he was seeing.

What he was hearing.

What he was **feeling**!

He then looked out and saw Gerald nodding in approval by the rear of the room. Dylan couldn't help but smile. He then pulled out his guitar again, as the crowd went absolutely hog-wild! After he reconnected the cords to everything he had broken down, he went to the microphone, and spoke proudly, "Ok, guys! Just one more!"

The crowd was screaming in adulation and approval. He then smirked and shook his head in disbelief, then began picking open chords. The crowd cheered and screamed at the sound, and Dylan began.

There's no more life on the north side,

That's all they say.

There's too many people,

in too short a time now

That said goodbye.

Now we've been sitting on the outside,

Just you and I.

We still have a dream, girl,

I'm sick of the real world

I'll be your eyes.

Nobody knew it, but Dylan borrowed this song from Sammie back home. Sammie had all the musical ability in the world if he would just **sack up when it counted,** and perform his music in the right spots. As Dylan had discovered, the "right spots" were in LA proper. Dylan figured that since he couldn't bring himself to be emotionally present enough in this moment to play his own music, performing a cover would be ideal. He knew that he couldn't play just any old cover. The crowd wanted to hear Dylan's originals! The way Dylan saw it, they wouldn't know this isn't his song, so it's fine.

Such a Charlatan!

Falling faster, as I pray.

Searching more for much to say

And all the things we fight for,

Does it matter anyway?

The crowd was going absolutely ballistic as Dylan belted out the trimmed down, acoustic rendition of Sammie's modern rock anthem from Philly. As Dylan catered to the crowd, in his classic Dylan-Stewart-style, they even began to sing along to the chorus, simple as it was.

"Heyyyyyyy!

Heyy don't cry!

Whatever comes and goes,

I'll ride with you!

Heyyyyyy!

Just dry your eyes!

Whatever comes and goes,

I'll ride with you!"

Dylan kept thinking about Parrish Street, and it made him sad. He continued the song through the next verse and chorus. Then he stopped and talked to the crowd. "Ok, now I'm not gonna play. We're all gonna sing while we clap, okay?"

He led them in that section but had to stop to correct their rhythm. "No, no... like this!" Dylan slowed the pace of the crowd to a very deliberate, powerful, mellow vibe. "That's it! Just like that! Now, sing!"

He turned the microphone to face the audience, and they all sang in unison.

"Heyyyyyyy!
Heyy don't cry!
Whatever comes and goes,
I'll ride with you!

Heyyyyyy!

Just dry your eyes!

Whatever comes and goes,

I'll ride with you!"

Now,

"I'll riiiiiide with you!

I'll riiiiiide with you!

I'll riiiiiide with you!

I'll riiiiiide with you..."

He stopped the audience by turning the microphone toward himself, and played the chords very softly and slowly, as he sang in a lower, more sullen octave, *"I'll ride..."*

He held the low note for a bit, then brought the guitar ringing to an end as he went vocally quiet. The room was in sheer anticipation. It was a marvelous sight. Dylan broke the silence as he said quietly into the microphone, "Thank you. Good night."

The crowd erupted in a roar of applause that he had never heard before in all his years of performance, of which there were **many.** The crowd stayed in attendance the whole time that Dylan packed up his equipment. At the end of the evening, he packed all of his gear into his Blue PT Cruiser. He heard someone approaching with singular applause. The applause was slow and deliberate, as though to hammer home a point. Dylan looked up from his trunk to see Gerald approaching his car. "That was **tiramisu** in a world of **eclairs**, Dylan Stewart."

The talk of tiramisu made Dylan miss his grandmother. She was an old Italian lady, so tiramisu is par for the course, eventually. Dylan always knew it was only a matter of time before tiramisu would be served somewhere! He quickly had to shake off this memory in order to respond to Gerald.

"You don't think I blew it with my early escape thing?"

"I was worried, to be frank. But when I saw how goddamned loyal these people were to you. That answered any doubt I may have had about you being a solo act. Dylan, I can offer you as much of the world as you are ready to conquer."

"Are you serious, Jerry?"

"I've never been this serious before. What I saw tonight spoke volumes to the marketability here! You're gonna be huge!"

It was everything Dylan ever wanted to hear.

Where do I sign?!

"Can you stop by my Santa Ana office tomorrow afternoon? I'm gonna write up paperwork to go over tonight. Sound good?"

"Yes, Jerry! That sounds amazing!"

After they parted ways for the night, Dylan returned to his apartment on North Vista. He brought his stuff upstairs and pulled out his phone, seeing that the notification symbol was blinking on its face. He flipped it open to see that a number that he vaguely recognized had called him four times earlier that evening. He also noticed one voicemail. He opened the flip phone, pressed the '1' and hit the call button.

Ring...

    Ring...

        You have One message!

           New message!

There was what appeared to be a physical struggle with the technology, then a frustrated pause, followed by, "Hello? Dylan?"

I know that voice!

Dylan felt a deep, sinking feeling in his chest, like his soul just fell inside of him.

"Dylan, it's your Uncle Carl! I know you're in Cali now, but you gotta come home! Your dad is in the hospital! Your mom is with him. Your brothers are doing their best to get there. I gotta tell you, Dylan. When I left his room there, I saw him have one. It was bad. I don't know if he's gonna be okay, Dylan! Call Sammie or Calvin or Kay. They have cell phones. Mine is gonna die. Okay, I'll talk to you."

....Daddy?

Chapter Thirteen: The Hanging Chad Outside of Philly International

"Where are you?" Kay said with immense panic in his voice. The panic seemed understandable to Dylan, given the serious and sudden nature of today's events. Dylan wasn't used to Kay being so tense and seeming to care deeply for Dylan's progress in his travels. Dylan just got right to it. "I'm on the flight back now, I should be at Philly International in about twenty minutes."

"Okay, I'll meet you there. Gate F, right?"

It bothered Dylan that the Kay he knew a few years back would have certainly seized the opportunity to make reference to Dylan's homosexuality based on the fact that he was pulling in to terminal "F".

" 'F' for Faggot, right? You British Cigarette, you! "

Something to that effect.

Or, no, wait! I got it!

*"You're **pulling in** to terminal' F', which stands for 'Fag-anus', right?" Yeah, that woulda been classic Kay.*

    Dylan had a telephone conversation with his dad a few weeks before, and Sam told Dylan not to worry too much about how distant Kay had seemed to him lately. Sam told Dylan that his brother had grown up quite a bit because of his job. He was now a manager at a property community and was a very accomplished, hardworking man. He had his sights set on an executive position in real estate or something. He even returned to Temple to receive his Master's in Business Administration.

    Dylan still didn't see how that meant that Kay needed to be a different person down to his very core. People loved Kay's assholery! It was his signature! The world would be different without it, and that made Dylan feel sadness. But Dylan abandoned his brothers to go pursue his own thing, so can he really feel some kind of way about things?

Dylan responded to his brother's timid, abnormally normal statement about picking him up at the airport. "Why are you meeting me there? I can prolly get a cab from the airport just fine. I don't wanna take you away from everyone, and from Dad."

"Yeah, it will be fine," he said with a strange pause, "I'll meet you there in 20. I'll be waiting."

"Okay, Kay. Thanks. How is he doing? What happened?"

Kay was seemingly distracted by something, or someone at the hospital. He then returned to the phone, quickly saying, "I gotta head out if I'm gonna get there in time. I'll see ya, Dylan."

Didn't really answer my question, but okay…

"Alright, Kay. I'll see ya soon! Tell him I love him!"

There was a pause, and Dylan was confused.

"Hello? Kay? You there?"

Nothing but silence.

Dylan pulled his phone away from his ear, and looked at the screen. The call had dropped.

We must be getting close to landing; I shouldn't be on the phone anyway.

Dylan put his phone away. The flight went on. He stepped off with his carry-on filled with a few outfits, his CD player, a book of CDs and a pad and pen, and made his way out of Terminal F. When he stepped outside, there was the standard audio track of the world of cars pulling into and out of the airport terminal area, and cab drivers clamoring for the attention of riders. Dylan did his damnedest to swim through all the sensory overload he faced. He saw Kay's luxury coupe parked in a loading spot. He walked over to approach Kay.

"Yo, man!" Dylan said, as he threw a handshake his way. "Thanks again for getting me, dude. Let's just get to him, okay?"

Kay received the handshake with one of his own, opened the passenger's side door for Dylan, then stood in the way of Dylan's entrance to the car, turning to face him with a serious look on his face.

"Look," said Kay with tears in his eyes, "He's gone."

Dylan felt the sky fall down around him and all the planes taking off from Philadelphia International airport seemed to crash, all at once. The cacophony of the "usual suspect" traffic around them fell into a sort of low, monotonous drone. He tried to speak, but how could he?

"What?!" Dylan choked out harshly. "What do you mean, gone?"

He knew what his brother meant. He was still somehow hopeful that it was not true. In actuality, Dylan was hopeful that his brother was back to his asshole ways of old, where nothing was off limits for a joke, "not even the Holocaust."

It was no joke. "I know. I know, man. He died."

The Stewart boys then got into the car. Dylan turned to face his brother in the front seat. "How's mom?"

"She's a fucking wreck! You know it man. I dunno how we're gonna do this! She can't be alone!"

Dylan knew exactly what that meant, even if it was not the intention of Kay at that exact moment. But he responded, "I know. I know. He was so young! What happened?"

"He had a heart attack at the house at dinner time last night. He made sandwiches for him and mom to watch reruns of the Simpsons, and she said he just passed out, right there in the bedroom."

"Oh my God, dude! What the fuck?!"

"I know, dude. I know."

Kay continued. "Then she helped him to the toilet and he passed out again, bashed his forehead on the edge of the tub. She showered him and everything before the EMT's took him out of the house...

...She's so fucking strong, dude!"

Amazing.

Amazingly sorry for her.

"Are the guys at the hospital? Did you all see him there, before…"

Dylan couldn't even bring himself to finish that sentence. It was like if he finished it, his father would be dead. Instead, the hanging chad just sat there...

Chapter Fourteen: What Became Of The People We Used To Be?

"You gotta come get your brother!" Midge screamed into the telephone. "He forgets who the mother is and who is the kid here!"

Calvin obviously did not want to deal with this nonsense. He had a lesson plan to make for his class for the week, and his own kids were giving him the usual hard time that they tend to give him on Sunday evenings, as the weekend is winding down. They could sense the dread of the new school week that was about to begin, and it felt like forever to them until they will see the light of day, even though it will only be five more days until the next weekend begins. Kids sure are stupid about time.

"Mom, he just cares about you a lot. We all do."

"Oh, fuck him, he 'cares' about me! He cares about **controlling** me. He thinks 'cause Dad isn't here, that this is **his** house! He forgets that your father had piss poor credit, and that it was from **my** job at the Mint that we were even able to **buy** this house!"

Calvin surely had heard this tale before. They all had. He attempted to bring the conversation back to the pertinent issue.

"Mom, look, we all know that it is the hardest thing you ever had to go through, Dad being gone and all. But you just can't drink it away!"

"I'm a grown person!" Midge shouted, accidentally spilling a can of Natural Light on the bedroom floor as she sprung up in her anger. "You will **never know**! I **pray** you never do!"

She was right to feel the way she felt. Sam and Midge were married for forty-two years when he suddenly and unexpectedly died. He was her whole world, especially now that the kids were all grown and moved away to do their own thing. They all had important things that they belonged to. Dylan ran away to start a new life in California. The others each had their own families. Moreover, they all had made something of themselves in their lives, and had career responsibilities to keep themselves occupied.

Sammie moved up to Scranton PA. It was there that Marywood University sat. It is where he had started his college career years prior as a music major. He fell in love with his wife in Philly, and they had a son. He had given up on his dreams of pursuing a career in music on stage. Instead, he did the much less sexy, much more responsible thing, and he began teaching music theory at a private university. It paid the bills and it allowed him to help to shape the next generation of musical artists, before they all have to make the choice to give up on their own dreams of fame and stardom for a more responsible, family-friendly situation. It is the "new American way."

Calvin finished his college career at Temple, then began his graduate studies elsewhere. He received a Master's in Early Education from Gwynedd-Mercy University. He fell in love with a beautiful girl that he met while working part time at a car dealership. Their love blossomed quickly, and they married and had two children. Calvin now taught at Cherokee High School in Marlton, New Jersey, which is where their family relocated for commuting purposes. He didn't much like the douchebag-ery of modern American high-schoolers, but the job was a perfect fit for his long-term goal of being a high school principal. So he regrettably had to move on from early education.

Kay, **oh Kay**... Kay topped them all. After mixing paint at Sears in his post Temple years, he got a job as a night security clerk at a high-rise apartment complex in Chestnut Hill. With grit and determination, he was able to quickly furlough that job into a management position. After becoming the building manager, he garnered the attention of another property in Perkasie, Pennsylvania. He worked there, running a luxury townhome community, and after a few years of "killing it" there, he was able to move into the executive track. After some success he received a job offer at a real estate development firm, where he worked his way up to become the company's vice-president.

The sky truly is the limit for that dickhead!

When asked about what changed for him from his Sears paint-mixing days (remember, in those days, he was genuinely excited about a Phar-Mor opening up adjacent to his workplace, so that he could drink Arizona Sweet Tea to his heart's content, and now he's a high-tier business executive with a fast luxury sports car and a wife and two kids of his own, and a big cottage in Vermont), Kay said, "I just had to grow the fuck up."

Fucking asshat!

So, clearly, the Stewart boys did not have to face their father's passing quite the same way that Midge had to face her husband's passing. So... she drank.

...A lot.

...A whole lot!

....Way too much!

After they left the hospital, Dylan moved in with Midge at her and Sam's rowhome in Northeast Philly. He was the first (and last) line of defense between jumbo cans of Natural Light and Midge's 5-foot 1-inch, 143-pound Irish frame. He hated being burdened by this responsibility. However, as he commonly shouted at her as he poured full cans of beer into the sink basin, "I lost Dad! I'm **not** gonna bury **you**!"

On this particular day, Dylan wished he had fought her harder about it. He gave up the fight after some four hours of shouting back and forth between them, and with her calling each of her sons to rat out Dylan for being an ungrateful, narc piece of shit.

*Oh, and calling all **thirty-eight** of her brothers and sisters too!*

Okay, not thirty-eight. That was a **slight** exaggeration. More accurately, there were five or six that she called every day to complain about Dylan's **iron fist**, which, remember—he *learned* by living with her.

Dylan sat on the motorized reclining loveseat that Sam had purchased for his retired life with Midge. His plan would be to retire from his career in the prison system and spend his twilight years watching **Family Feud**, **CSI** and **According to Jim** with Midge until they died, likely holding one another's hands as they did. It sounded like the fairy tale existence that is marketed to audiences on the big screen and in pop music for all time.

Life—and **fate**—had other ideas. Sam was dead. Midge sat in their marital bed watching reruns of Home Improvement and whatever other malodorous and insufferable slop she could find. She sat alone. Well, she was joined by cans of Natural Light strewn all about her. She laughed, at times. She cried **most** times. She occasionally put her hand on top of the dent in the Sleep-Number mattress that had been carved out by Sam's dad-bod over the last several years. She would lovingly caress the dent, occasionally saying, "I miss you, boob!"

And then there was Dylan. Sitting by his lonesome, in his father's living room, with his PlayStation 3 hooked up to his father's 44" flat screen television. He remembered how excited Sam was to tell Dylan about the TV that he had purchased. Now, he knew that it wasn't the biggest, most luxurious television set on the market. That didn't matter. It was **Sam's** Television! He knew it the moment he laid eyes upon it while shopping for groceries and such at BJ's wholesale food market.

"Your mom and me deserve this TV, Dylan!" Sam enthusiastically shared.

"Your mom and **I,** not **me.** Are you a **caveman? Me deserve this TV!**" Dylan just had to correct his father's English.

"Oh, kiss **me** ass, Dylan!"

*God, I'm gonna miss **him**!*

As Dylan reminisced about giving his dad a playful, but hard time about sentence structure, he heard a very sudden, very loud crash come from inside his mother's bedroom. He threw down his controller and sprinted to the room to see that Midge was lying almost upside down in the closet on top of their Doberman/Rottweiler mix, Sergeant. That dumb dog was just fine. He just seemed rather bothered by his mommy collapsed drunk on top of him. She winced in pain from the closet.

"Oh my God! Are you okay, Mom?" Dylan asked as he hustled over to her and grabbed her hand to assist her to her feet. After one failed attempt to support her own weight, Dylan realized that he was there and no one else was. So, he would need to remedy this situation himself. He then supported her behind her knees, and hoisted her upward. When she was stationary in his arms, he carried her to her bed.

"No, no. Bathroom..."

Ugh.

"Okay, let's go." Dylan helped her to the bathroom. He thought to offer her assistance getting situated there, but she said, "I **got it**. You can go."

"Are we going to talk about this? This is your **third** fall this week! I can't lose you too, mom!"

"Just **get out**. Get out of my **house**. **Get out of my life!**"

Wow. Okay. Gloves off!

Dylan shouted back with disdain for his mother's words. "Are you **fucking kidding me** right now?"

"**Get out! Get out! Get out!**"

"I'm going to play the game and you can just sit on the floor of the closet next time, **drunkard!**"

Dylan would regret that sentence every minute of every day for the rest of his life. The rest of the night, he played the video game in the living room. He noticed that his mother had gotten her old breathing machine (an oxygen-assistance device), and carted it off to the room. She hadn't used it for about 2 years before that night. Dylan knew this because Sam told him with **great** excitement when she stopped needing to use it. He was so relieved. It seemed as though they had finally beaten her COPD for good. That, again, was two years before that evening. On that evening, she felt the need to use it again.

In the morning, Dylan went in to check on Midge. She was taking very labored breaths, and winced in pain as she was doing after the fall the night before.

"Are you alright, mom?"

"No. I think you should call 9-1-1."

In Dylan's experience with his mother, she would normally exhaust **every** possible option before involving a medical professional. Midge was very old school. Those folks thought they could remedy *any* medical situation, ailment, or emergency **on their own!** Often times, those remedies required makeshift devices made from household supplies. Dylan and his brothers would always refer to her as Dr. Midge MacGyver, MD!

This must be for real!

Without hesitation, Dylan called for an ambulance. As they carried Midge off on a stretcher out of the house, Dylan called his brothers to tell them all. He got through to only Sammie, but left voicemail messages for the other two. Dylan then drove to sit with his mother in the infirmary.

When he got there, he checked with her doctors. They informed him that she had broken several of her ribs and collapsed a lung. They would reinflate the lung and see how things went.

Dylan again called his brothers. Like before, only Sammie was reachable. Dylan stayed at the hospital alone until Sammie showed up. Over the next few hours, Kay and Calvin arrived. Over the course of the next few days and nights, Midge's status would improve and drastically decline almost spastically. Over time, she got worse and worse, as both lungs collapsed.

Midge slipped into a vegetative state. She was largely unreachable, though visitors' voices caused her face to move as though she was trying to smile but just couldn't. It was the hardest thing the Stewart boys ever had to witness, and Dylan thought of what Sam's final moments must have been like.

At 2:43 PM on a Wednesday, Midge passed away. Dylan held her hand as she passed. He was shocked that he could actually **feel** the moment his mother's soul departed her body. Kay was also in the room. Kay was always her favorite. Dylan never thought it was fair. See, of the Stewart boys, Kay was the one who most closely resembled Sam as a young boy. Well, as Kay grew, the correlation between their facial appearances continued. Dylan would always insist to his mother, "That isn't **fair**! He looks like **boob**!"

Of course, Dylan wasn't claiming that his loveable dickhead brother and best friend resembled a woman's **breast**! You *know*? *Boob*? The silly pet name!

"She's gone?" Kay asked, delicately.

"Yeah," Dylan said, unsure of how to respond.

"I *felt* her go, man!"

What became of the people we used to be?

Chapter Fifteen: The Restless Need Rest

Sammie and Calvin sat on the couch at Dylan's house on Tyson Avenue. Midge had written a living will after her husband had passed to ensure that Dylan had security. Her thinking was that her other three brothers were all happily married and owned their own nice houses with their wives and children, so she would make sure that Dylan was secure in his life should she, for whatever reason, no longer be here.

What the Stewart boys realized then—that they were **fearful of** the very moment their father died—is that their mother no longer had any motivation to be alive. It broke them all to their very core. Dylan was *fortunate* enough to have been reminded of her pain day-in and day-out once he moved in with her...after leaving his recording contract hanging unsigned in Los Angeles to bury his father.

Dylan didn't think twice about the decision. She was the greatest mom in the world, and she would have gladly dropped everything in her life if Dylan needed her to do so, so when the **shoe** was on his foot, he wore it. She even asked him to leave her and go back to LA and perform again. This was maybe two months after Sam had died, and before she started really self-medicating heavily in her grief, which in turn made Dylan her biggest enemy on Earth, as he tried to prevent her impending death.

"You did the right thing before and chased the Hollywood life! From what you said, you *had* it. Just go back and **get it**."

*But **Jackie** is avoiding me, and that is why I gave up Philly. And because of that, I killed Daddy. Soon, I'll kill you too. I can't let that happen! So, I'm staying here, and that's that.*

Dylan knew he would never put those feelings into words to anyone. It would be his festering burden to sit with for all time. And also, he doubted highly that he could now deliver a performance that a guy like Gerald Dunphy would still demand of his talent. However, now that she was gone, his brothers had their concerns about his ability to properly care for the house and the responsibilities that came with home ownership. Their hearts were in the right place, though it still bothered Dylan to no end.

"You want a beer?" Calvin asked as he rose to his feet.

"Yeah, thanks bro," Sammie responded. Calvin came in from the kitchen and handed him a Yuengling Black and Tan.

"Here you are, Sam."

Sammie took the beer with delight. "Thanks, bro!" He sat back down after rising to grab the bottle and continued, "So, Kay is almost here, right? When is Dylan gonna be back again?"

"Yeah, Kay just got off 95. He's in town for an office opening. They went national."

Sammie was rightfully impressed with the progress that his younger brother was making. He wanted to address that briefly, but kept his excitement about it to his vest. He knew that focus was necessary tonight. He inquired again, "So, **Dylan**?"

Calvin answered quickly and confidently, "He said he'll be back by 6:30 and we can just wait here. That's why I called you over. I have a key, remember?"

"Yeah, I get it. You think he'll be on time?"

"Well..." Calvin said with a smirk while shaking his head, "...I wouldn't **bank** on it. That guy is late to **everything**. He was late to Mom's funeral **and** he was late to dad's! He is **gonna** be late to his own, I swear!"

Sammie chuckled lightly and retorted back, "He **has** to be better, man!" Calvin nodded in agreement. They both said, almost at the same time, "Let's hope!"

Just then, Kay arrived at the opened front door.

"Kayyy!" called out Sammie. "Congrats on the expansion!" Kay opened the door with a confident smile, and said, like a dickface, "Yeah. We are **killing** it, man!" *Such a cock.*

"Big things. **Big things**."

Calvin laughed and walked to sit down on the couch. He then asked his younger brother, "So, you have the finance spreadsheet, right?"

"Yeah," Kay said as he opened his briefcase, "It took me two hours last night to go over that dude's taxes! He didn't pay property taxes 3 out of the last 5 years? They are gonna **take** this house from him. Guess he'll be homeless then; cause I'm not taking him to Vermont."

Sammie started in with another pressing issue to discuss, "Are we gonna talk to him about his arrest? Cause he hasn't kept a job in the last two years, and he has been blowing through the inheritance money in his savings to pay the utilities." Sammie said with great concern in his voice, "And now this charge he's facing. I just worry it's all gonna crash and burn."

"What's gonna crash and burn?" a voice said through the screen door. It was Dylan. He had returned home, and overheard the tail end of the conversation. He knew they were all coming over to discuss some things, he just wasn't exactly sure what they would be addressing.

Dylan entered and went brother to brother shaking hands. He hadn't seen Kay in person in about 5 months now. There was a family funeral that they all attended in Conshohocken, and a luncheon that followed ('cause nothing helps death go down easier than braised beef and sautéed mushrooms).

Dylan saw Sammie last month at a house party. He wanted to fuck Sammie's wife's best friend **so** badly, and she was gonna be at the party, so Dylan put on his *white shoes*. This was despite her husband picking her up afterward in their luxury sedan. He was a doctor... and a lawyer... and a maintenance chief... a decorated war hero... and likely a magician.

*Yeah, **definitely** a magician.*

Dylan saw Calvin about three weeks ago. He had tickets to see veteran standup comic Norm MacDonald perform at a casino, and he knew his brother Calvin was a huge fan. It was a fun evening, though Dylan was disappointed he didn't get to meet Norm afterwards. For some reason, Dylan always did his best to meet every comedian he saw live after their set, and normally, he had a pretty high success rate. They had no such luck with Norm, however. The show was still fantastic, though.

Dylan ended that night having meaningless, dirty, depraved sex with a waitress from the casino bar. Yes, sex in general **should** be a *positive* thing, and is viewed as such by most men. But Kimberly was **not** Jackie. She **wasn't** Lara Feldmeister. Instead, she was just the next willing succubus.

He absolutely **longed** for Jackie. He couldn't look into a girl's face without seeing Jackie's eyes, and little nose, and rosy cheeks, and sparkling demeanor. It was eerily similar to how he had been obsessed with Lara Feldmeister for all those years. The only difference was that with Lara, he couldn't sleep with other girls. It is one of the reasons he stayed a virgin for as long as he did. But after he crossed *that* bridge into manhood, so to speak, he had found sex to be an oddly therapeutic replacement for strong feelings.

Dylan spent years bouncing from one girl to another, trying to **fuck** his way to happiness. The issue was that he would *never* find happiness in another person if he couldn't first find it in himself. It took him years of depravity to be taught that lesson by a psychotherapist he began seeing as was ordered by Philadelphia municipal court.

"So, what is this all about?" Dylan asked his brothers. Kay spoke up first, turning a file and a long, yellow pad with his black ink strewn all about it; the figures and bookmarks were readily apparent.

"You really need to get your shit together, man!"

"Look, you guys have no idea wh—"

Sammy interjected loudly, "**No**, man! **You** have no idea! We can't watch you falling through like this! You are drinking too much!"

Dylan shouted back in anger, "Oh, get the fuck outta here!" He began to tear up as he shouted, "I was **begging** you guys almost **every fucking day** to help with Mom. You didn't want to be bothered. And now, **she's fucking dead!**"

"You can't put that on us, man," Calvin said in a calming voice. "We all wanted Mom to cool it. But she **lost her world**, man. So, we let her be, and deal with what she was dealing with in her own way!" He put his hand on Dylan's shoulder. "I know you did your best, bud. And we all appreciate it, but there wasn't anything **any** of us could have done for her!"

Kay then spoke up, changing the conversation back to the fiscal side of things. "Look, man. You've got to pay these taxes on the house this year. When you put yours in, talk to Reich about it, okay? He'll be able to help you with a plan to get caught up. There's no choice here, man. They will **take** this house!"

Fucking City of Philadelphia!

"So, is that everything?" Dylan asked impatiently. "My drinking and my money?"

Calvin and Sammy looked at each other, then Calvin began. "Persephone wanted me to talk to you about something."

"Yeah, what's that?"

"Well, it's about your arrest. She is worried about you being around the kids."

"What the **fuck**?" Dylan said with frustrated confusion.

"You gotta understand, you are facing charges for **harassment**. A girl called the cops on you because you kept visiting her house, even after she asked you to stop."

"I'm not a stranger or anything! I **knew** her! She is Jackie's best friend! I figured she would have some knowledge of what Jackie is up to now. They were *so* close!"

"*Molly?*" asked Sammie, genuinely trying hard to remember the girl's name.

"No, Jackie's friend **Lily** from Temple."

"Did you ever meet her before she said you were harassing her? **Lily,** I mean?"

Dylan was clearly frustrated by this line of questioning. "**Of course,** I met her. She was at the Draught Horse at Temple to see SVG."

"And you talked to her then?"

"Of **course** I did. I asked..."

Wait, um...I don't think...

Dylan let out an audible sigh. "No."

"**No**?" asked Calvin with serious doubt about his brother's frame of mind.

"Well, yeah. I—I saw her at the bar. Jackie was with me near the other side of it, she pointed out... she... pointed her out to me. It's how she was visiting, she was crashing with Lily in Tacony!"

Kay spoke up, sounding like an expert litigator. "You're going to jail, dude! You sound delusional. I'm just telling you how the court is gonna see your case. You spent **all** of your twenties making enemies of long-time friends. And **all** you do consistently with your life is drink whiskey. **Oh**, and fuck randoms. **That too**! You pay your taxes when **you** feel up to it. Perception is reality, my man!"

"I have a case, guys! Lily is just a fucking **liar**! How do you think I found out that Jackie went back home? Lily told me she went back!"

"You don't have any other witnesses to this? What about Steve? Ryan? Did they meet her?"

"Who, Jackie? Yes, of course they did, we went to the frat together."

"No, not Jackie, you **ass**! Lily! Did they meet her?"

"They had to have..."

Audible sigh, again.

"...I don't really remember. It was so long ago."

"Hold on," Kay said, pulling out his phone and walking into the kitchen. After about three minutes, he came back. "Ryan is coming over. He'll be here in like 6 minutes. He has a house on Lardner now."

"I haven't talked to him since..." Dylan got oddly reserved, then continued slowly. "...oh man, it's been a while."

Kay responded with vitriol in his voice, "Since you **fucked Sarah**? In **his bed**?"

Dylan was still so ashamed, but he had to respond, at least to save face in front of Sammie, who was unaware that Dylan gave the dick to his best friend's ex-girlfriend.

"Dude, they had broken up! I'm telling you! I was drunk, and hurting, and I was watching his dog for him while he was down the shore. She came over and knocked...

...Was I supposed to shut her out?"

"Yes, numbnuts!" Calvin shouted at him, then shook his head in disbelief.

"I let her in, she used the downstairs bathroom. She came out topless! And she has double D's! You woulda done the same!"

"**No**," Calvin said firmly and deliberately, "Bros **before** hoes, buddy! Have we taught you **nothing**?"

"I guess... is he gonna fight me again?" Dylan asked Kay curiously, "'Cause I hated fighting him last time, but he slugged me, and I wasn't just gonna take it."

"You should have. Maybe he'd still be your friend. Cause he was your best one! Whatever happened to Steve?"

"Ah, Steve. Funny guy!" Dylan got up and got a beer from the fridge, came back and sat down on the couch again, then continued hesitantly. "I messed up with him too, guys. Can we not really talk about this anymore?"

Sammie retorted eagerly. "No, Dylan, I wanna know. **What** did you do?"

"I had sex.

... With Kaitlyn."

"Wait, his girl?" Sammie asked with sadness is his eyes, disappointment on his brow.

"Oh, Dylan."

"No. No. They broke up two months before that. He cheated on her and she left him."

"But still, dude! **Another** bro? Stationed in line behind **another hoe**?"

"I know, I know."

"Wasn't it worse than that?" added Kay.

Such a cock!

"Yeah," Dylan said, then took a deep, labored breath, and came to the conclusion. "It was a threesome with his sister too."

Calvin and Sammie sounded as though they had heard enough. Calvin, his frustration at his brother's actions brimming to the surface, spoke up angrily.

"He shoulda fucking **killed** your stupid ass!" He then added the cherry on top. "**I** woulda done it **in his honor!**"

"I was young! And it was a *total* dream dude! Like a scene from a porn!"

Kay speaks up again, "You weren't **that** young, dude! It was four years ago!"

"Was it? Oh man, time flies when you're doing absolutely nothing of value."

"Yeah, so look, man, you can't come over our place in Marlton anymore. Not until this legal stuff all sorts itself out," Calvin declared. "...You gotta understand that."

"I don't, but it's fine..." Dylan continued, "...It'll be over soon."

The doorbell rang. Kay walked over to open the door. It was Ryan. He walked in and handshakes went all around. Well, until he got to Dylan, and there was an awkward moment between them. Kay saw it and interrupted it with the purpose of this visit.

"Ryan, thank you for coming here on short notice. As I said on the phone, we need to get to the bottom of the Jackie and Lily situation before Dylan's hearing on Tuesday morning," Kay said while opening a different legal pad from his briefcase. "Now, I know you guys aren't friends or anything anymore, but I just need to know if you ever met the plaintiff in this case? The woman, Liliana, is alleging that Dylan kept visiting her place and harassing her for information about Jackie from Los Angeles."

Ryan grabbed the hair hanging over his forehead with his open palm in frustration and said "**Oh, God,** this **shit** is still happening?"

"What do you mean, Ryan? What do you know?" Kay said as he prepared a new page with his precise rolling-v gel ink pen up to the surface of the pad.

Ryan furiously and frustratedly shouted out, "Jackie **never fucking existed!**"

The room then fell silent and still, with the brothers shaking their heads and looking toward Dylan with sincere concern, or whatever the fuck. Dylan was not silent and was not calm. He sprang up out of his chair angrily.

"Don't you **fucking say that shit**, Ryan! She went to the Sigma-Phi-Epsilon party with us! I left to bring her back to Lily's! If she wasn't there, where the **fuck** did I go? And **who the fuck** did I fight with the devil about not fucking because she was too drunk?!"

Dylan felt the eyes all on him. It was not his favorite party activity. Not at all. All he wanted to do was leave. But **he** lived in this house. None of *them* did. He had no idea what to do, so he did the only logical thing. He stormed to the kitchen and reached on top of the fridge. There, he grabbed his fifth of Johnnie Walker

Black-Label scotch whiskey and headed for the front door. Sammie stood in front of it, not letting him leave. He then did the next best thing. He headed for the basement stairs. As he turned back toward the kitchen, Sammie called out to him, "Just stay here and talk to us, Dylan! We love you!"

Dylan had a one-track mind; he was done with this conversation. He turned back to his brothers and Ryan. "Just lock up when you leave," he said, annoyed. "I'll be around."

"Dylan," Calvin said with a calm, but determined voice. "You can't run from this stuff, man!"

"I'm not *running*. I'm just clearing my mind." Dylan went down the stairs and left through the back door. He then walked with his whiskey onto Bustleton Avenue and to Frankford Transportation Center and took the train into the city. He ended up walking on Parrish Street with his open bottle of smooth, top shelf elixir. He drank it and drank it, never chugging it. He sipped it and enjoyed the flavor delicately. He loved the prominent notes of peat and smoke in its flavor profile. As he sipped and walked, he found his way out to the front of his childhood home.

His phone rang.

Jackie??

He looked at it, with dismay,

Kay.

He answered the phone. "Yeah? What's up?"

"My friend Chris wants to represent you Tuesday. He's gonna meet with you tomorrow."

I don't need a lawyer, dude!

"Why should he represent me?"

"He has never lost a case on Filbert before! You **need** his services, dude! Just be quiet and let him do what he does!"

"Whatever, dude."

"The hearing is Tuesday. He will get you off. His office is closed Wednesday and Thursday for New Years. He said he wants you back in his office Friday, okay?"

"Why?"

"I'm not a lawyer, dude. Let him do his thing, please."

"Okay, that's fine..." Dylan finished his bottle and headed back to take the train home. Later that night, in his tired, groggy, whiskey-soaked state, his mind began to race...

*How dare **Ryan** pull that shit in front of my brothers! I know I hurt him and all! But certain things are uncalled* *for! He used to be such a great dude! I miss when he was **this** Berg!*

Dylan lay in bed, staring up at the ceiling. Long ago, he moved into his parents' marital bedroom. He got rid of their bed, of course. He couldn't bring himself to sleep where they used to sleep. He did his best to remake their home into his home, but that house would always be theirs, and he knew it. As he lay there, two days away from facing criminal misdemeanor charges that could possibly take away his rights as an uncle, he could only think of one thing.

He reached over to his phone.

He pushed buttons.

The phone rang.

The phone rang again.

The phone rang for a third time.

He waited, eagerly anticipating the voice he needed to hear. The phone rang again, for half of a ring, then he heard a slight click, could it be?

"Hello, Jackie??"

There was a momentary pause in sound, then her voice began. It was her, singing.

And even though the moment passed me by,
I still can't turn away.
Cause all the dreams
you never thought you'd lose,
Got tossed along the way.
And letters that you never meant to send,
Get lost or thrown away.

And now we're grown up orphans,
That never knew their names.
We don't belong to no one,

That's a shame.

If you could hide beside me,

Maybe for a while,

And I won't tell no one your name.

And I won't tell 'em your name.

This is a new voicemail! Another new voicemail! See, Ryan??

And scars are souvenirs you never lose,

The past is never far.

Did you lose yourself somewhere out there,

Did you get to be a star?

And don't it make you sad to know that life

Is more than who we are?

We grew up way too fast,

And now there's nothing to believe.

And reruns all become our history.

A tired song keeps playing on a tired radio.

And I won't tell no one your name.

And I won't tell 'em your name.

I won't tell 'em your name.

Mmm, mmm, mmm

I won't tell 'em your name, ow

I wish I didn't lose you, Jack...

I think about you all the time,

But I don't need the same.

It's lonely where you are, come back down,

And I won't tell 'em your name.

After the beep, Dylan opened his soul. "Jackie, I know that I fucked things up. I always have. I always will. But

I want you to know, that even still, no matter what happens, meeting you was the highlight of my life. You are the **best** thing that ever happened to me, Jackie! I love you, and I am **so** sorry!"

Dylan wasn't sure where he was going with this. He decided to close it out. "I've said I'm sorry by now, at least once, to just about everyone!"

Dylan hung up the phone. And there he lay. Looking at the ceiling in his parents' bedroom, watching the old, dusty ceiling fan that hadn't worked for as long as he'd lived there.

The restless need rest.

He would find none.

Chapter Sixteen: Was LA Worth It?

Dylan sat in the courtroom next to Kay's friend, Christopher.

"Your honor, it would be irresponsible to punish my client for these accusations. Firstly, Mr. Stewart has *never* done anything illegal in his **entire** life. He never even received **detentions** in school as a child!"

"I understand that, Counselor. But your client did, in fact commit a crime here if these allegations are proper and true. We cannot turn a blind eye to harassment charges! Harassment is a very serious offense and can be the tip of a much larger iceberg."

"Your honor, forgive me for saying so, but that in and of itself is speculative at best. Also, your excellency, if I can also play a bit of the speculation game, it can be assumed that the plaintiff isn't all that fearful for her own safety from Mr. Stewart. If you would notice, Ms. Phillips failed to even *appear* here today to see first-hand that this so-called *justice* was even **done**! Also, if you will turn your attention to the defense exhibit A-2, we argue this is at best a case of simply mistaken identity. My client has **no** interest in bothering the plaintiff. He never had interest in her *whatsoever*. He was after a mutual acquaintance. Ms. Phillips didn't even go into detail in her filing of charges, she merely wanted to sick the dogs on Mr. Stewart, and I am not sure exactly why, but that does not matter."

Chris continued confidently. "Now, your honor, it is incumbent upon you to make an example of this claim and set a proper precedence. Otherwise, who knows how many other plaintiffs will clog up this already crowded court docket with these maliciously erroneous claims! Let my client walk, sir!"

Kay was right about his friend. What he lacked in truly litigious savvy and expertise, he sure made up for in his ability to persuade with his words. After a small recess, the court reconvened, and that is where Dylan sat now, awaiting his fate. Dylan was a total ball of nerves as the Judge began to address the courtroom. Dylan stood up next to his attorney. All he wanted to do is drink whiskey and listen to records. The judge's voice bellowed out over this big upstairs court room at Philadelphia Municipal Court.

"Mr. Stewart," he said. "I've made my decision."

Panic.

Sheer panic.

Gulp

"Yes, your honor?"

"Mr. Stewart, I find you *guilty* of Harassment in the 3rd degree."

The world is over.

"*However*, since this is your first offense, and I personally do not view you to be a danger to Ms. Phillips, I hereby sentence you to 1 year of probation, starting today."

Probation.

Cool.

Probation.

*I'm still a **criminal**!*

Fuck!

When they stepped out into the hallway, Christopher seemed disappointed. He addressed Dylan. "That's the first guilty verdict I've gotten while doing this! It **ruins** my record!" he said, before noticing the look of fear on Dylan's face.

"But, hey man," he said, "it's only probation. It's not even a stay-at-home order! You won, man! A guilty verdict for 3rd degree is 6 months jail, minimum."

"Is it?"

"Yeah, Dylan, it is. So, you're a very lucky man! Think of all the shower abuse you just escaped!"

He did have a point there!

"So, what? I have to report? What's this all mean?"

"I'll have you in my office tomorrow to go over the mandates. I wasn't gonna come in, but it can be quick. Does one o'clock work?"

"Yeah, it should."

"Alright, I'll see you at my Chestnut office."

"Ok," Dylan said, before adding, "Thanks for everything, Chris!"

"Your brother bailed me out so many times, man! Thank *him*!"

Such a cock!

Dylan was sitting at his house, waiting for his brothers to arrive. It had been about a month since his meeting with his lawyer. A month since he found out that he had to do voluntary reporting every month with his PO, and also had to start seeing a psychotherapist. Karen was his therapist's name. He had seen her three times this month and would see her again on Wednesday of that week. She helped him to get in touch with a lot of his personal struggles with acceptance. Turned out he just needs so badly to belong to *something*. It is what his backyard wrestling federation was all about. It's what every single Little League organization he'd ever been a part of was about. It's what his friendships were all about too. She seemed to focus a lot on the dynamics of his friendships with Ryan and Steve also. She even found a lot of meaning in his dreams. He was **crazier** than you would ever think him to be.

There was a knock on the door. He answered it.

"Hey, man!" Sammie said. "Calvin is coming from the car, so hold on."

His older brothers arrived. He asked them, "Is Kay gonna be here?"

"Yeah," Calvin said, "He better! He has the info to go over!"

"I'm fine!" Dylan insisted to his brothers. "I'm better!"

"We know, man! We know! You just need to stay on top of the financials! That is what he wanted to meet about."

"I ordered from Pizza Roma," Dylan added. "You guys hungry?"

"I'm *always* hungry, dude," said Sammie. "Thanks! What do I owe you?"

"Don't worry about it! I had a good week!"

"What happened? Are you working again?"

Gulp

*I can't tell them that I've **sucked dick** to be able to afford my utilities this week. They would **flip the fuck out**.*

...*Well,* **utilities and**...

Dylan went and grabbed the bottle of Johnnie Walker Black, poured himself a tumbler-full, and began to sip as he spoke up. "Yeah. I found a few odd-jobs on craigslist."

Ok, not a lie.
The guys **were** *odd!*
Sucking dick for money **is** *a job!*

"Oh, that's cool, man!" said Sammie. Unbeknownst to him, his little brother had been whoring himself about town using Craigslist personal ads to find clients.

He tried to get work legitimately. **Every** time he got to the orientation stage of the hiring process, or before it, his arrest and his probation came up. And every time, he thought to himself, "*I'm so **tired** of sucking **dick**!*"

Just then, Kay arrived. "What's up, **jailbird**!" **Such a cock!!**

The brothers sat around the dining room table. After their pizzas arrived, Dylan got paper plates and napkins, all paid for with blowjob money, of course. Then the "meeting" began.

"Shows here your monthly expenses to live here are 1200 dollars. I told you it's illogical and irresponsible to keep dipping into savings to stay afloat."

"Yeah, I know dude! What do you **want** me to do?!" Dylan shouted back, "**Suck dick** for **money**!?"

Sammie then spoke up, "No one is sucking dick for money, dude."

*Oh Sammie. Sweet, unaware Sammie! Your heart is **so** pure!*

Dylan reached into his pocket. What did he find there? A **lie**! "I know, man. It's a **joke**!"

Smooth. No more jokes, Dylan!

Kay then put on his **big boy** pants again, "I think you gotta get rid of FIOS. You don't need TV, and there are much cheaper internet options. Even better, the library is three blocks away, and there is **free** Wi-Fi there! Use the computer lab!"

Such a cock!

"I need my HBO!" Dylan retorted. "It's not TV... It's HBO!"

Kay, as per the norm, was not in a joking mood, "It's not a fantasy," he pooped out into the air, "It's real life."

I don't think that would work as a slogan!

"I'll be fine, man! Really, I will just keep finding odd jobs, and keep paying bills, and I'll be fine," Dylan said. "I got this! Really! I do!"

"I don't think y—" Calvin interrupted Kay, and said in his signature cool, calm, Barack Obama-like voice, "If he says he's got it, Kay, then he's got it. He's a grown man. Let's trust him."

"Yeah, I know, but if he doesn't pay the ta—..."

"I'm **gonna** pay the **mother-fucking taxes**, ya dick!" Dylan shouted angrily.

After an awkward pause, Kay continued his piece. "Are we gonna discuss the *lost girl* thing? Or is it too soon? Are we still treating it like she existed?"

His two older brothers tried their best to minimize the flamboyant response they expected from their youngest brother, but to no avail.

Dylan sprang up and punched Kay right in the eye. "She's not a fucking **joke**! **She is real**! She was a better friend to me than you **ever were**, dude!"

What ensued was an epic, four brother fist fight that no one ever expected to happen. When Kay returned fire to Dylan, and Dylan wouldn't stop the ascension, Sammie pulled Dylan off of his brother, so Dylan slugged Sammie. This caused Calvin to slug Dylan. Dylan loved a good fist fight, so this turned into a scene from Street Fighter. By the end of it, Kay left the house angrily, with briefcase in tow, followed by Sammie and Calvin. As he was leaving, Calvin turned to Dylan and said, sternly, "You **gotta** get your shit together, dude! I'm serious!"

Having started down the front steps, Calvin leaned back over his shoulder, adding, "You're gonna end up **all** alone, man," before making his final point:

"Was LA worth it?"

Chapter Seventeen: Gone Again...

Dylan couldn't bring himself to finish watching the rest of the happy celebration scene at Times Square. After all, for the first time in his life, he was feeling totally confident about a declaration he made. Did it worry him that *this* particular declaration was to take his own life?

To be totally transparent, Dylan wasn't exactly fearful of death itself. It is more what happens **after** that wasn't sitting well with him. He was haunted by his mother's sage testimonials and teachings.

"Suicide is for cowards. And there is no spot for you in Heaven if you kill yourself, because you took God's greatest gift and you just threw it all away. You're basically spitting in God's face! So, why would you be given access to eternity in heaven?"

"Mom, I thought that God was very forgiving. As such, if someone is hurting that badly that they just want out, so they kill themselves, wouldn't God understand and forgive them? Isn't **that** the whole point of *all* of this?"

"Dylan, you're eight years old. You'll get it when you get older. I promise. Just know that suicide isn't an option, okay?"

Dylan was forever haunted by those words.

Suicide isn't an option.

Why are we not allowed to do with the gift of life as we see fit? I get it that God can't just have people killing themselves on a whim. I get it. But if life is a *gift*, shouldn't it be up to us what we **do** with that gift? For instance, if your Uncle gives you a pack of baseball cards, but says that you can't open them up, ever, because they will depreciate in value, isn't that a fucked up gift? Just get me a **fucking bike**, Unc!

It was now 3:01 am on January 1st. Dylan had long since turned off New Year's Rockin' Eve, and he was playing games of Madden on his PS4. The phone rang in his pocket.

Jackie?!

He looked at the screen. A 213 area code.

213?

Hollywood!

Jackie?!

He pressed the green answer button on the screen of his iPhone. He had kept the same cell phone number and transferred that number to *several* different cell phones over the years. He had to.

He answered. "**Hello??**"

The other side of the phone call was very noisy. There was much commotion going on in the background. He couldn't wait any longer.

"Hello?? Jackie??"

Then, in perhaps the single greatest moment of his entire life, the voice on the other end responds. It is that sweet, soft, delicate and angelic voice that he has longed to hear since 2002.

"Dylan?!"

Oh my God, it's her! Praise Jesus, it's her!

"Jackie?! Is that really you?"

"Yes, Dylan, it's me!"

Dylan didn't know exactly how it happened, but he burst into tears. Those tears provided the greatest relief he had ever felt. In all of his years of depraved sexual exploitation, he had never had an orgasm that was as powerful as the sense of relief that he felt right now, on the phone, with Jackie. He attempted to compose himself. "Jackie, what happened to you? Why did you run from me for all these years?"

"I'm sorry, Dylan. I wasn't ready for you. I was fighting against it back on Mulholland, but when I couldn't stop thinking of you, and worrying about you, I came to Philly."

Then Jackie got very forlorn, "And when you told me about you and Jessica, it completely broke me in two."

"I'm so sorry Jackie! I had no idea you felt for me like that! You have to understand, if I knew I would have never left you at Lily's."

"What?" Jackie asked in a very puzzled tone. Just then the crowd noise behind broke into a cacophony of joy. It sounded like the greatest New Year's party there had ever been! After what sounded like a struggle on Jackie's end, a man's voice began. His voice was ominous. Somehow it sounded so familiar to Dylan.

Was it Charles Hogan?

...Was it Judge Berkshire-Smith?

...Tony the Taxi driver?

...Skitch?

...Was it one of the homeless?

...Was it **Kent, the barkeep**??

"Hey, Dylan! Jackie isn't feeling well. She'll call you later."

Don't do this to me! Please! Not again!
Not this time!

*Oh, **come on**!!*

Dylan was in a panic, imploring the familiar stranger not to take her away from him again.

"Please, man?

Just let me talk to her.

Just a minute more?"

That seemed reasonable enough. Just then, Dylan heard the most painful noise he had ever heard in all his years. The phone clicked. All of the background commotion. The party. All of Dylan's hopes. All of his joy.

Gone.

Just like that, **Jackie was gone**.

                                                  ... Gone again.

Chapter Eighteen: It's perfect

"Why don't you try to return to school?" Sammie said. It had been roughly four months since Dylan spoke to any of his brothers at all, and he was shocked that Sammie even called him this evening. "I don't even want to be—", Dylan started, before quickly deciding on another topic of conversation. He continued, "Why are you even calling me, dude? I haven't even been here in 3 months."

"Where **were** you, man?"

"I took a train to Chicago, then to LA."

"**Again, dude**?!" Sammie shouted through the phone at his youngest brother. "**Why**, man?"

"You know why!"

"So, did you find her?"

"No. I couldn't track her down. I gave up after getting chased out of her old job again. I came back home after that."

Sammie sounded very bothered by his brother chasing a girl who may or may not even *exist* across country...

...again.

He continued on, "Coming back was the right call, man. I'm sorry you're going through this. We've all missed you, Dylan."

"Yeah, okay," Dylan said dismissively. "Miss you too."

Yeah, okay...

"You know Christmas is next week, right?" Sammie said, before extending an unwelcomed invite

Dylan's way. "I'm getting you guys and the kids together for dinner at our new place in Warminster. I want you to check out the new area! And you gotta see how much Polonia likes it! She's getting along with all the kids in our neighborhood now! It's the best set up we've had in a while!"

*Oh, yeah, Christmas....there's **no** way I'm gonna be sad there!*

"That's great, man. I'm glad she's happy there." Dylan was happy his niece was finally happy. She was *so* goddamned smart. But Dylan remembered (from when he was very smart) that other kids don't often like that very much. Dylan then pivoted the conversation abruptly back to the dinner idea.

"I'm not really gonna celebrate this year, man. I'm sorry. I can't."

"Don't be like this, Dylan! You know Mom and Dad would want us to still get together every year for it! We gotta!"

"I can't, dude! Not this year! My head isn't right." Dylan then thought of another idea for this coming week. "Look, Sammie, I gotta roll. I have a job to do in a couple hours. I am still two months behind on the utilities after paying off the first two months I missed in LA. I'll catch up with you later, man!"

"Alright, dude, I'm here if you need me, okay?"

"Alright, Sam. In case I miss you, happy holidays! Give Antonia and Polo my best!"

Dylan hung up, he then looked online for information about the ball drop at Times' Square in New York City on New Year's Eve. It wasn't until mid-March that he remembered the lone resolution that he ever made in his life, which he made last New Year's Eve. When he made that resolution, he was thinking he would kill himself any day after that. Then Jackie **called** him! He then had a new-found hope that he could find her again. But when he went across country without a plan...**yet again,** only to have a similar lack of luck as last time, he was out of options, and he came back to Philadelphia.

He had been struggling to think of a fitting suicide to commit. One that is dramatic enough to justify the tragic story of Dylan and Jackie. When Sammie called him, it reminded him that he is almost out of time and opportunity to off himself this year, which he must do. It is the principle of the whole thing. Remember, he never made a resolution because it becomes an obsession that you chase all year. And it has the potential to ruin your life if you fail to reach your goal. Even an already ruined life shouldn't be harder still. But now that he made a resolution, he knew he simply **must** do it this year.

    The plan was now in mind.

    New Year's Rockin' Eve. On air.

    Gunshot wound to the head. On air.

    On stage.

    That will be how it happens.

    It will be nationwide news.

    Jackie will see the story.

That'll show her how much I cared about her!

Perfect logic.

Perfectly planned.

The perfect ending of our love story.

The perfect ending of my life.

                                    ... It's perfect.

Chapter Nineteen: A Resolution to Die For

"Is this your first time here?" a woman in her 30s says to Dylan, as they are both standing in a very long line in Manhattan.

"Yes, the website said to head out 6-8 hours earlier than I hoped to be here to get a better spot. I left Philly 7 hours ago, and here I am, stuck in this sea of frustration like everyone else!"

Dylan thought that he might want to remember to leave even earlier next year. Wait, if things go according to his plan, there will be **no** next year.

Dylan had his satchel, which contained just four things:

1. A trusty book of CDs.

2. A note pad.

3. A precise rolling-v black pen

... and the last item was the toughest for him to find before his trip. Considering that the end of the year kind of snuck up on him, he didn't have time to put his name in for proper clearance or anything. Instead, he had to visit the not-so-pleasant area of Kensington in North Philadelphia. At a boarded-up home near a freight-train railway there, close-ish to Somerset station, he was able to purchase a small, black Beretta 92FS.

    This handgun was certainly not intended for what Dylan planned to use it to do. The Beretta FS is a military field-tested combat pistol that allows for seamless rapid fire. It would be a helpful piece for Dylan if he was using it against enemies at Times Square. However, his only target that night was himself. In his defense, he knew very little of guns in general, as he had been against gun ownership his entire life. However, shit was about to get real.

"The line is moving pretty well now!" Tori offered, with hope abundant in her tone.

"Yeah, I'm not getting my hopes up. It's like someone, somewhere is try to keep me from doing this tonight!"

*Do you mean God? Mom? Dad? Fate? What the **frig**, man?*

Tori volleyed his serve right back to him, "You can't talk like that! You're gonna get there! And you'll do this tonight! This will be scratched off the old bucket list!"

If only she knew what was in this satchel.

She continues, "Do you have one?"

What, a satchel? Yes, right here!

A gun? Why, yes! Also right here!

Is tonight finally my night to shine?

*'**Tis**, Tori!*

*'**Tis**!!*

 Just then, by her anticipatory silence, Dylan could tell she needed a response.

 "I'm sorry, what?" he offered politely.

 She laughed, and heartily said, almost in a scream, "A **bucket list**!"

 Dylan then thought of his first night in LA. Wow, so much had happened as a direct result of that night. Because of that first night, in eventual terms, both of his parents were now prematurely deceased. He felt tremendous guilt for both of their deaths. Because of that night, again in eventual terms, Dylan now had a criminal record, albeit a minor one. Also, as a result of that night, again in eventual terms, Dylan was once offered a recording contract by a big time music producer, and he never signed it, followed up on it, or even spoke with his prospective producer ever again. How **could** he, after he had to **bail** with no hesitation to return home to bury his father? Also, as a result of that night, he had absolutely no friends or family by his side in his life any longer. But things **do** happen for a reason.

"Where is home for you, Tori?" He didn't actually give much of a shit what her response was, it was one of those questions that we just have to ask as people to keep conversations going. Especially when a conversation serves a purpose, such as this one did. See, without this conversation, Dylan didn't trust his ability to stick to the plan, as he might have gotten a head start on the whole suicide thing.

It was a strange feeling. He knew there **is** no tomorrow after today. There are no minutes after the minute he pulls the trigger. No moments beyond that one. Tori, taken aback by his question, hesitated, then responded in her signature southern drawl, "I'm from Muskogee, Oklahoma".

"Wow. How is it there?" Dylan asks, even though he remembers his time there during his ill-advised return trip out west.

"Oh, it's home!"

What kind of a bullshit response to an honest question is that?! I know it's home. To you! And a lot of other slack-jawed yokels! Keep my mind off of what I'm about to do!

"I hear it's dusty there," Dylan said with a chuckle.

"Yeah, I 'spose it is!"

"I love your accent, Tori!"

I actually hate that accent!

It's such a vibrant sound!"

*A **vibrant sound**?! What in the **name of holy hell** are you **saying**?!*

"Oh, ain't you sweet?"

Aren't you?!

How close are we to the ball?!

    Dylan looked around where he and Tori were standing. He caught a glimpse of a street sign. He saw now that the crowd they are standing in has been drudging along 38th street. 7th Avenue was just ahead of them. Dylan knew from mapping out the route earlier in the week that the ball would be dropping at One Times Square, which is right near the corner of 42nd and 7th.

    This scene is something that Midge wanted to see up close all her life, but never did. See, Sam and

Midge were willing to take the kids just about everywhere when they were young. Well, everywhere within reason. And given how wiry the Stewart boys were, Midge always thought twice about the trip to Times Square on New Year's Eve. Dylan thought to himself for a moment,

Well, mom! I'm here now!
Not for long... but I saw it!

*And I'll **forever** be a part of this night!*

As Dylan and Tori reached the corner of 7th avenue, they began to veer in the direction of the source of all the commotion. As Dylan beheld the wide-open Times Square from afar, with all the fluorescent and neon lights, the flashes of photography, the roaming vendors, the street performers, the human robots with fedoras, the Scooby Doos and Elmos, he turned to his new companion, saying in amazement, "Tori, this is the most beautiful sight these eyes have ever seen."

Dylan couldn't help but think of sitting on Sam's knee watching **Rudy** for the first time. *Great movie. Great moment.*

Tori smiled, and laughed, as she returned the sentiment, "I feel you right there!"

As they got closer, Dylan could make out some of the images that showed on the big screens around the neighborhood where they walked. These screens showed footage from many different locations around Times Square, as well as shots from scenes around the world at this very moment. He was craning his neck around a corner to see one such high screen that sat atop one of the buildings in Manhattan's Theater District. What he saw simply shocked him to his very core. He saw Ryan Seacrest, replete with his ghost-jizz hairstyle, interviewing guests. There were several people waiting in a small line behind him, each awaiting their opportunity to shine on this grand stage. He couldn't help but to lock his eyes upon the sixth person in the row behind Seacrest. He would recognize those beautiful baby blues anywhere. A beautiful blue—azure; like they were from a dream he once had. The rosy cheeks—like a famous painter used her porcelain skin as a canvas. The tiny nose—almost like that of an adorable baby pig, or something. He knew that he had found **Jackie**.

He couldn't help but to angrily think of the allegations thrown at him by Ryan at his house the night of the fiscal intervention.

She is real!

... And wait 'til she gets a load of what I have to show her!

The line was moving much quicker now. Dylan was overwrought with excitement. What will he say to her? Anything? Or will actions work better tonight? Dylan reached into his satchel and pet the barrel of his Beretta. Just then, he felt a tug on his shirt sleeve. He turned to see that Tori was standing with a goofy looking rube, dressed in what Dylan was sure is the usual attire for a gentleman from Muskogee, Oklahoma. Tori spoke up joyously. "Have a great time tonight! Be safe, sweetheart! Ya hear?!"

"I hear! I hear! You too, guys! It's been real! Tori, trust me, you will never forget this night! For as long as you live! Enjoy!"

You sick motherfucker, Dylan! You're gonna ruin that poor girl's life!

*It **has** to be done!*

As Tori and Rube Rubenfield took off in the other direction through the crowd, Dylan felt panic as he spun to look for a screen. He found one and saw that Ryan Jizz-hair was still there. Jackie was now the fifth in line. Dylan took out his CD player and loaded the perfect song for this stupendous moment in his demented life. He figured he had time for the perfect song to set the mood while he walked the few blocks left to get to the stage. It was a live piano recording, and it hit him deep with the first line.

They're waking up Maria

'Cause everybody else has got

someplace to go

She makes a little motion with her head

Rolls over, and says she's gonna sleep

For a couple minutes more

I said I'm sorry to Maria

For the cold-hearted thing

that I have done

I've said I'm sorry by now, at least once

To just about everyone

    Dylan could only think of Jackie, sitting in her room in LA, checking her voicemail, hearing Dylan utter those words to her.

She says, "I have forgotten

what I'm supposed to do today"

And it slips my mind

what I'm supposed to say

We're getting older

and older and older and older

And always a little further

out of the way

You look into her eyes

And it's more than your heart will allow

In August and everything after

You get a little less

than you expected, somehow

As the song went on and Dylan got closer and closer to his final act, he began to panic again, as he thought about the possibility of missing yet another chance to talk to Jackie— to **be with** Jackie again; the fear he felt rushed over him until he realized that Jackie hadn't moved up in her place in line.

*That must be some celebrity or something he's talking to right now. Thank God for **Billie-Jo Armstrong**, front man of Green Day!*

Dylan kept on moving forward toward his moment of fate.

They dress you up in white satin

And they give you

your very own pair of wings

In August and everything after

I'm after everything

Midge died on August 15th. She was far too young, and far too strong to die. She didn't realize it, but she gave her life for Dylan, in the eventual sense of the term. Dylan knew that, and Dylan regretted that every day of his miserable, dick-sucking, whiskey-drinking, bill-avoiding existence.

Just then he caught a glimpse of the screen and saw that Jackie was now third in line. He checked his phone. He sees that it is 11:10 PM.

You're still good...

...You got this!

...This night is yours!

Well, I got my reservations

And I got my seven-million dollar home

I got the number

of some girl in North Dakota

Who's always wide awake

So I never have to spend the night alone

I got this nasty little habit

Of peeking down the shirts

of all the little girls as they pass me by

And I know you wonder

when it all catches up to me

And they finally bring me down

Do you think I'm gonna cry?

Well listen, I already got my disease

So get your fucking filthy hands

off of me

I hope you weren't expecting me

to be crucified

The best that they can do is just to

hang me from the nearest tree

Dylan then looked at a different screen, to see that Jackie was now second in line.

Not today, Satan!

Dylan then paused his Discman and began to run. Well, he ran about as much as the moment and the population that surrounded him would allow. But he didn't care about being rude. He had more of a right to reach the stage than any of these folks do. He arrived at the rear of the stage where Jackie was waiting to be interviewed by Ryan Ghost-jizz Seacrest.

Dylan then used his limited knowledge of event staff security practices to ascertain the best route to Jackie. He hoisted himself up onto the rear of the stage.

It appeared as though no one has noticed his arrival there, until he heard a deep, angry-sounding voice from his rear. "**Hey pal!**" it bellowed out with thunderous bravado, "**You can't be up there!**"

Dylan then heard the menacing noise of radio chatter between guards, which Dylan took as motivation to move with more vigor and purpose. In his haste, his giant headphones had slipped loosely down around his neck. He darted towards the front of the main stage. He could hear the sound of Ryan Seacrest's made-for-TV banter growing louder and louder, the closer Dylan got to his Golden opportunity. He felt an excitement that he had never felt before in his entire life.

Just as he was feeling this new feeling of joyous tension, he was immediately hit by the worst feeling he had ever even imagined were possible to feel. He felt as though something has burst deep inside his soul, and it was followed by an immense heat that radiated throughout his upper body.

He then felt a clubbing blow from his left side. It is one of the guards for the ball drop festivities. This big oaf struck Dylan from the side like he was Brian Urlacher and Dylan is Lions' running back James Stewart, no relation. As it commonly did for James Stewart, it didn't end well for Dylan Stewart, as he was taken down in a heap, on his face. The impact slammed Dylan's discman into the on position. It actually had restarted the song entirely. So the ambiance for this scene was playing around Dylan's neck for this entire collapse scene. Dylan laid there on his face, clutching his chest. It was the worst pain he had ever experienced in his life. This was a level of discomfort that he would not wish upon his most bitter rival. The guard who tackled Dylan realized what was happening. He called for help on his radio, and a small ambulance pulled up, right next to where Ryan was conducting his interviews.

Fuck!

His interviews!

Jackie?!

Dylan tried his hardest to lift his head up enough to see down to the front area of the stage, where the Ghost-jizz hairdo was currently bobbing in place. He couldn't see a line behind him though, as the line may well have been over his other shoulder, thus out of Dylan's line of sight.

Fuck me!!

Just then, a paramedic began to speak to Dylan. He could barely see his face, though he could hear his voice very clearly, which is strange, given the location. There was an utter cacophony of New Year's nonsense all around right now, yet this paramedic was speaking to Dylan. And every word is crystal clear.

He **knew** this man. **He knew this man well**. He could not believe that he was being helped by **this** man, right here, right now. Dylan felt so at peace, it is absolutely shocking to him. He had given up all of this sort of thinking, given up all of the bullshit that he had caused in his own life over the years. The paramedic he knew spoke to him in a voice that was so eerily familiar that Dylan could not stop himself. He began to cry, as he heard, "**I told you**, your pop-pop had his first heart attack at 26!"

This can't be!

What?!

The?!

Fuck?!

Is?!

Happening??!!

Just then, the paramedic leaned over top of Dylan, and suddenly, Dylan could see his face so clearly.

"**Dad**?!" Dylan was choking through his tears, as he smiled at his father, and said, "Dad, I'm **so sorry!**"

Sam looked at him and smiled a warm smile, then said to him, "Why, Dylan? You did what we always told you to do! You followed your dream. Whatever dream that was. It didn't matter how illogical it was or how wrong it seemed to everyone but you. It was **your** journey. You made it **yours**. We never stopped being proud of you, *especially* **your mother!**"

Dylan had never felt that kind of peace before in all his years on this Earth. He then asked the only logical question to ask your father when you are unsure of your situation. "What's gonna happen, daddy?"

Sam wiped a single tear from his eye, then looked right into Dylan's eyes, and spoke the words no father ever wants to say or hear. "Son," he said, placing his hand over top of Dylan's chest, "You're gonna die."

This is it! Here and now! This is all behind me!

"Okay, dad. I'm ready," Dylan said, before he was reminded of something he couldn't possibly forget. "**Wait**!" he shouted out. Sam leaned in closer to Dylan as he responded, "Yeah, Dylan, what is it?"

"Dad?" Dylan asked in the sweetest voice he could muster, "Was **she** real?"

Sam looked down at his youngest son with a slight smile on his face, and told him, "That is for **you** to decide." He then gestured toward the front of the stage with an open palm, as if to present the scene to him. "Look."

Dylan rolled his head over toward the front of the stage. A crowd had amassed there, around Ryan Seacrest. Everyone was looking at the scene of the paramedics working on Dylan. In many ways, it was everything he wanted it to be. He saw, standing just behind Ryan Seacrest, the rosy cheeks, blue eyes, a piglet nose that he yearned for all this time. She looked right at Dylan. He smiled a soft smile and waved his best presidential wave at her.

"I love you, Jackie!" he mustered, on his back on the stage as the paramedics worked on him. He looked back to find his dad's face, but no longer could see it.

Dad?!

I'm here!

I'm ready!

Come back!

Please?

Then, everything quickly began to get very dark, and he realized his fate was sealed. The music played him out.

In August,
and Everything After,
I need someone else
To bleed for me...

Chapter Twenty: A Fitting End

"I used to know you, when we were young,

You were in all my dreams.

We sat together, in period one.

Fridays at 8:15..."

Stew did his best to shake off the all-encumbering grip of sleep as he smacked the screen of his phone to silence "Hackensack" by Fountains of Wayne. After bassist and co-founder Adam Schlesinger died of complications from the Coronavirus (Covid-19) on April 1st, 2020, Stew set his ringtone and daily alarm tone to "Hackensack," which was their best song. He did this in remembrance of such a great song-writer. Adam actually had written the song "That Thing You Do," from the Tom Hanks/Liv Tyler flick from the 90s of the same name, about a band's rise to stardom in Erie, PA in the 1960s.

Stew always loved that movie. He especially loved the scene where the young bandmates first heard that their song was playing on the radio.

Oh, the joy.

Stew lifted himself out of his bed. He loved how comfortable his bed was. It cost him close to 1600 dollars, and it was the first order of business for him after his mother passed away. His parents left their Northeast Philadelphia rowhome to him, and it was now in his name. And as hard as he tried, he could not seem to make himself comfortable attempting to sleep in his parents' bed after they were gone. He broke their bed down and discarded it on a trash night near the end of August, some two weeks after his mother died. He then slept on the couch until his new queen sized Nectar bed was shipped to him.

Stew had tough choices to make after the house became his. He **hated** this house. He hated everything about it. He hated how tiny it was. He hated how odorous the house became over time. He lived there alone with his parents' two huge Pitbull dogs. They were old dogs. One was roughly thirteen, the other is the first one's son, and is almost twelve. Stew fed them and washed them, cleaned the yard after they did their business, frequently. However, Stew had made it clear to his older brothers that he will not *ever* take them to the vet... **ever again**.

"At their age," he argued, "and at their sizes, and their genetic make-up, getting a doctor involved is just playing God."

"So, you're just gonna let them die?" his brother would say.

"Well, yeah. I mean, they're not sick. When they get sick, they get sick. I'll make them comfortable. But it's not up to me at that point!" He continued on, "What? I'll go broke paying for a surgery? For what, three more months of life before they *naturally* meet their maker?"

He had it all figured out.

He had recently decided, on a whim, that now would be the right time for him to return to school. He thought it might be a good experience, and it might be good for him to challenge himself to finish his degree, especially now that his folks had up and died.

If only they could see me walk across that stage! Man, that'd be sweet!

He had been back to school for a bit now. He finished his first semester back and did much better now than he ever did years prior, before his life choices robbed him of a promising future. He then decided to stick with it, and see it through. He also did well in his second semester, despite the fact that the *entire* world was **shut down** because of the death of the guy who wrote "Stacy's Mom".

No, really, the world was shut down in the Spring of 2020 because a guy in China decided to eat a bat, and it got him sick, and he spread that sickness to a bunch of people, who spread it to their friends and families, and so the World was closed. It's called a Global Pandemic.

Hopefully, these are a thing of the past sooner rather than later, but I'm just not so sure.

Anyway, about school. It bothered him how difficult things were for him now. It bothered him how difficult it was to be taken seriously by his fellow students. He was literally **twice** as old as many of his classmates, and in this new #METOO culture, it was inherently complicated for a young girl to be anything *but* creeped out by an older gentleman trying to be nice to her, albeit with no sexual undertones whatsoever.

Logic would dictate that he should have just started to interact with young men, instead. You know, 'cause young men aren't influenced by a movement like #METOO, right? **Wrong**! He found in his first semester back that most of the young men in his classes wanted nothing to do with an old guy who had a hard time communicating to their douchebag minds. So, as he has grown accustomed to do in his life for quite some time now, he was facing school **alone**.

All alone.

He finished his Cracklin' Oat Bran, threw away the cardboard bowl and plastic spoon and filled up each of the dogs' food and water bowls. He then went to his room and made sure the door is locked, so the dogs leave his **fucking** mattress alone. He grabbed his MacBook Pro, put it in his laptop case/backpack, and began his tedious trip to Temple University. He knew he had to stop at the computer lab first to print out the final piece for his final portfolio in his Creative Writing course. The Workshop was filled with so many "*judgey*" young people, that Stew never really felt comfortable sharing his material.

"No one seems to get me, teach!" He implored his professor, "Maybe I should just drop it?"

"That is *entirely* your call! But I like your stuff. A lot. And I think you should stick with it! This class is a real "Get-What-You-Give" sort of thing, Stew," Courtney said, as she closed a folder on her desk in her upstairs office at Anderson Hall.

"**Ha! The New Radicals!** I **fucking** love it!" he shot back, laughing, "Ok, I'll see it though! What's the worst that can happen?"

"Great, Stew! This is exciting!"

What he wouldn't have given to fuck his professor right then and there! She was 3 years younger than he was, but much closer in age and maturity than the other non-options he experienced daily! Also, she was **cripplingly** attractive to him! Yes! It's a thing!

Today, he wore a mask on his face. The world had re-opened, but now everyone had to wear masks that covered their mouths and noses, to limit the spread of the airborne virus that had killed so many already and would likely kill even more before the world was able to figure out a better way to combat it.

He entered the lab to see that everyone there had surgical masks or bandanas covering their faces. It was like a scene from a poorly made western/medical drama, if that genre exists.

Was Dr. Quinn a Western character?

Well, kind of?

It was post-Civil War, Colorado, right?

Close enough!

Yeah. Stew walked onto the 2020 version of Dr. Quinn. He found a computer. He printed out what he needed to, and he added it to the rest of his portfolio material. He then made his way to the elevator. He was **super** nervous about this.

I hope that this is enough.
*This **should** be enough.*
*This **better** be enough.*

The elevators are packed, as usual. Though everyone is wearing a mask, there are many people who are waiting for the next elevator, so the line is quite large. Eventually, Stew makes it onto an elevator with four other students and one faculty member. There is no possible way to remain 6-feet apart, as has been prescribed by society since this pandemic took hold of daily life.

This doesn't fucking matter.
Not today.
Just let me upstairs!
I can't miss class today!

Stewart reaches the eleventh floor and makes his way toward the room where his workshop meets. He hears the usual sounds of pomposity emanating from within.

Stay clear.
Stay focused.
Just get it done.

He enters. Courtney is standing behind the podium in the front of the room. The class is only a little more than half-full, even though the elevator situation has caused Stew to arrive twenty minutes into the workshop.

"We will get through everyone today, since the full class isn't in attendance. After today, you will not need to come back. We're done! Congratulations, guys! You've reached the finish line!"

As Courtney was waxing on about the accomplishment of successfully completing a writing workshop course, Stewart began to panic slightly.

I hope they like it.
*I hope they all **get** it!*
I hope this was enough.
.... for someone...

*... for **anyone**.*

Courtney had continued, likely for a while, as Stew was lost in his thoughts. The class was all stopped and looking at him, sitting in the back row of the workshop near the windows that overlooked North Philadelphia outside. There was an air of anticipation, and Stew panicked that he missed whatever it was that caused them all to look at him. He focused fully on Courtney's stunning good looks, as she stared impatiently at him. Now was his moment...

"Oh, I'm sorry, Courtney!" he musters. "What did you say?"

There was a light chuckle throughout the workshop, as Stew felt many eyes judging him harshly at that moment.

Courtney offered, "Do you have your final piece to submit?"

"I do," he said nervously.

"Do you want to stand up?" she asked him vibrantly. "The floor is yours, as they say!"

Stew then heard a voice that he knew from somewhere. It was a voice he hadn't heard in quite some time.

"The floor is yours!"

He stood up with his satchel over his shoulder and walked to the front of the class. "I'd like to lead the discussion from here, if I may."

Courtney obliged and stepped away. She actually joined the rest of the workshop in the audience, as he began. He was **so** nervous. He was as nervous as he had ever really felt at Temple before. He began, lacking confidence in his voice.

"My piece, as you know, is called Resolution," he said, as he took out his portfolio to remove the chapter at the end of the piece. His hand was actually shaking as he began to discuss Dylan's trip to see the ball drop at Times Square.

*They're not gonna feel **you**, man. Just bail.*

"Um... uh..." he stammered as he panned the faces of the room. They were all so damned judgey. As if to say, *"Come on, Stewart! We're waiting!"*

He continued, *"ah...*
I j-ju...

... D-Dylan goes..

... h-he sees.

... you're just not..."

The voice from earlier returns, loudly, almost at a shout.

*"The floor is yours, **man**!"*

Once he heard this, he looked over the indignant faces of the workshop, all snickering to themselves about this poor, tortured 37-year-old shell of a man...

... with no friends...

...With estranged brothers

... And **dead** parents...

...And ex-**wives** (plural).

And for the first time he could remember, he felt confident. Like nothing could stop him.

He said to his audience, "I wish you would have worn raincoats." As he took the Beretta out of his satchel, he began to sing.

In August and Everything After,
... I need somebody else
... To bleed for me.

After the loud bang, screams filled the entire 11th floor of Anderson Hall.

Anderson Hall was where he met Jackie.

Anderson Hall was where he realized that his parents are no longer here, and that it is entirely **his** fault.

Anderson Hall was where he started to come to terms with the fact that every single romantic relationship he has ever been in has failed because he had been hopelessly in love with a specter from his past. A girl that was in his 6th grade English class that he had never even kissed before.

It was Anderson that brought him so much clarity.

It's only a fitting end that his brains would be blown out all over his workshop in Anderson Hall today.

There were no more voices daring him to act.

There was no more guilt that he was never the superstar that everyone had always believed him to be.

There were no more cryptic, overwrought song lyrics.

There would be no more lonely nights being haunted by living alone in his parents' home.

There was no more doubting his purpose.

There were no more second and third and fourth chances for him to ultimately fuck up.

There were no more blown saves in the bottom of the last inning.

There were no more thoughts of what might have been.

There would be no more living for fearing the wrath of God.

There were no more unattainable expectations to justify.

There was no more chasing resolutions...

...There was no more broken heart.

I'd like to thank you for reading this story. It started when I was a young man and it became the series you've read after a lifetime's worth of lessons were learned. I hope that you enjoyed the story of Dylan Stewart, and I hope it spoke to you (and I hope that you GOT it). Thanks again! Take care of yourself....as though no one else will! I love you...

Made in the USA
Middletown, DE
24 November 2021